Nothing but *Ghosts*

Nothing but Ghosts

BETH KEPHART

LAURA GERINGER BOOKS
HARPERTEEN
An Imprint of HarperCollins*Publishers*

HarperTeen is an imprint of HarperCollins Publishers.

Nothing but Ghosts
Copyright © 2009 by Beth Kephart
www.harperteen.com

Library of Congress Cataloging-in-Publication Data

Kephart, Beth.
    Nothing but ghosts / by Beth Kephart. — 1st ed.
        p.   cm.
    "Laura Geringer Books."
    Summary: After her mother's death, sixteen-year-old Katie copes with her grief by working in
the garden of an old estate, where she becomes intrigued by the story of a reclusive millionaire, while
her father, an art restorer, manages in his own way to come to terms with the death of his wife.
    ISBN 978-0-06-166796-1 (trade bdg.)
    [1. Grief—Fiction.   2. Loss (Psychology)—Fiction.   3. Gardening—Fiction.   4. Research—
Fiction.   5. Mothers—Fiction.   6. Art—Conservation and restoration—Fiction.]   I. Title.
PZ7.K438No   2009
[Fic]—dc22   2008026024
                                                                                                      CIP
                                                                                                       AC

Typography by Carla Weise
09 10 11 12 13   CG/RRDB   10 9 8 7 6 5 4 3 2 1
❖

First Edition

In memory of my mother

Nothing but *Ghosts*

Chapter *One*

There are the things that have been and the things that haven't happened yet. There is the squiggle of a line between, which is the color of caution, the color of the bird that comes to my window every morning, rattling me awake with the hammer of its beak. You would think that the glass would break, or else that dumb bird's beak. You would think that I could think myself right on back to sleep, because I am sixteen, a grown-up, and I know things.

But this is the start of every day: being rattled awake by the world's most annoying bird.

"Hey," I say, sitting up in my bed, smoothing the hair from my face. "Cut it out." The finch pops me an odd look, then hammers some more. I say, "Go." It goes nowhere. I stand and press my nose against my own side of the glass, but that bird just hangs there, just hangs there and hammers. "What is *with* you?" I say, then flop back down across my bed. I can't smother the noise with my pillow.

It is only six fifteen. A little patch of my brain feels like sizzle, but if I close my eyes now, I'll never get to work on time. Downstairs an orange is being peeled; I can smell it. The coffee machine has gone into its huff-and-steam routine, and I picture Dad and how he'll be—his extra-large T-shirt hanging down past his boxers, his super-nerdy glasses catching the sun that comes in through the window above the sink. He'll have the newspaper spread out on the table like a cloth, his hair sticking up like rooster feathers. In the morning Dad is not what anyone anywhere would ever call pretty.

"You're kind of freaky looking," I decide to inform him.

"House only needs one beauty queen, Katie," he says.

Our house is too big for us, and also too old. Even when my mother was alive, I would feel lost in the oversized rooms with the dark furniture that had been here forever and ever. It is an heirloom house, passed on by my mother's mother, whose own mother (there is a picture in the stairwell) had gotten married on its lawn. Years ago someone painted the red-brick facade white, and the white remained, flecking off in places beneath the ivy but thick most everywhere else, so that even in summer the house looks like it has been caught in a late-winter storm.

Across the driveway from the house is the

studio—converted stables with an office up on top and a gigantic, open room below, which is where my father works on the paintings he restores. He sits there with the special lights beaming; the jars of resins and gesso on a wheeled white table; paintbrushes in coffee cans, vases, pencil holders; the stretcher wood stacked like tinder; the big, crinkling rolls of Mylar leaning into a corner. People come from all over to see my funky-looking, super-nerdy dad. Paintings arrive by crates, in trucks, on canvas rolls—favored paintings, paintings with stains and tears, paintings smoked all over by a fireplace fire or left in somebody's basement, forgotten by everything but the thick, black mold. He studies what comes through his pairs of glasses—the thousands of pairs that he wears on his head or around his neck when they aren't on the bridge of his nose.

"You only have one pair of eyes," I reminded him once.

"Yeah, but so much smoke and time to see through," he said.

My dad has this knack for lighting the darkness, for uncracking all the cracks that break images apart, for returning the disappeared to the land of the living. Except for Mom, who disappeared just three months after she'd been officially diagnosed. Three months. Ninety-something days. Science, chemistry—that couldn't save her. Preservation genius counted for zip. Extra, extra-special eyes had no impact. I blamed Dad for a while, and then I stopped. He'd loved Mom more than anything. I'd seen that for myself.

My mom vanished the day before Christmas, and of course there was no Christmas after that. There wasn't my birthday, which was February. There wasn't Easter. When I won the high school essay award, Dad took me out to lunch, and that was nice and sweet and all, but Mom? Mom would have filled the house with peonies, because peonies are the world's sweetest, dearest fat flower. They have personalities, Mom said, and feelings—the red ones bold and the peach ones shy and the purple ones adventurous. That was Mom's opinion, one of the zillion things about which she was sure. She'd call her flower news up the stairs for me to hear, then go out to the studio to tell her favorite art restorer.

You can't be as alive as Mom was, and then be dead. You can't be singing so that your voice fills every room in a hand-me-down house, and then not be heard at all. The math doesn't work. I went kind of crazy with the wrongness of it for a while, and then Dad and I talked and he said he knew no cure, the only thing he knew was the power of staying busy. I took on more school projects. I joined more clubs. I stopped hanging out so much with my two best friends, Jessica and Ellen, because I didn't feel like explaining, I didn't want to answer their questions or to feel their pity. I got a job at wacko Miss Martine's estate the day we finished finals.

Dad works on the paintings ten hours a day, then makes like a master chef at night. He isn't really a master, and you can't call him a chef, but he reads the cookbooks and he chops and he stands at the stove and stirs. "What're you making, Dad?" I have learned to ask him.

"The best roast chicken you've ever had," he'll say. Or "Hamburgers au gratin." Or "Barbecued pork not a second past juicy." I roll my eyes. He doesn't care.

My job is cleaning—the roasting pan, the basting brush, the cutting board, the carrot tops, the stalks of the Italian parsley, the plates, the silverware, the grill. By the time I'm done, Dad's on the couch, in the dark, in the blue light of the TV, where he falls asleep half-way into David Letterman's Top Tens. He won't sleep in his own bed now. I'm the only one on the second floor, and yes, sometimes I hear the sound of flutter. It isn't the bird and it isn't a bat. I haven't bothered Dad with this fact.

But right now it is morning, and Dad's pouring three or four tiny Rice Krispies into a gigantic bowl of milk. He's pulled a soup spoon out of the silverware drawer and is standing, the bowl to his chin, at the sink. Four Rice Krispies in an ocean of white.

"There are chairs, you know," I tell him, and he grunts. "Sitting's civilized," I say. He shrugs. I tug open the refrigerator door, draw out a can of lemonade, pluck an apple from the crisper drawer, then stuff both into the canvas backpack that clings to my back like Sammy Mack, the little kid across the street. Dad and I call Sammy "Monkey," because that's just what he is. You look up, he's in a tree. You stoop down, he climbs on your back. He's only four, and I told his mom he's headed for the Alps. Either that or the Olympics. His hair is red, the color of flames. His eyes are tiny specks of blue.

"Dad," I say now, "I'm taking off."

"Don't work too hard," he says.

"Don't forget your glasses," I tell him. As if he ever could.

"Don't forget your lunch." Yeah, right. Not even an outside possibility.

My bike is the ten-speed, thin-wheeled kind, a perfect silver streak. If you were looking down on me and my bike from a cloud above, you'd think we were a zipper. That's how fast we go, how straight down, all the way to Miss Martine's.

Chapter *Two*

Gardeners are crack-of-dawn people. That's the first rule. You get into place before the sun starts sulking beneath the trees, while there are still cool, dark, shady spots. The best shade at Miss Martine's is alongside the watercress stream, and that's where we gather every morning to get our list of chores from Old Olson. What needs weeding, dividing, thinning, staking are the things Old Olson knows. There are year-rounders and then the summer staff, and I'm the youngest, but not by much, and today, Old Olson is saying we'll be divided into two. Families, he calls them. Rest-of-summer kin. "We have got ourselves an excavation project," he says. I'm assigned to the dig.

You have to cross the stream to get to the site. You have to walk across the stones, then make one big leap for the banks, and I'm the last to get across, the shoelaces of my work boots trailing in the leafy watercress, a turtle swimming beneath my shadow. I know that there's nothing much on the other side but stonewall crumbles and the busted blues of fat hydrangeas, because I was here yesterday, all alone, listening to the water flowing.

Ida has plopped herself down on the edge of the crumbled wall, her big face and squished eyes catching a cone of slipped-between-the-trees sun. She wears a smashed hat on her fluff of gray hair and shorts that stop too high above the knee. "This would be layers of history right here," she declares, from her stone. She likes to think that she knows everything.

"This would be make-work," says Reny, who is the other long-timer and so scary thin that his pants seem tied on. Some people say that Reny is Ida's man, but I only ever see them bicker. Of course, Danny and Owen argue all the time too, but that's different because they're brothers, practically twins. Danny is headed to college in the fall, taking his big head of lemon-colored curls to Boston U. Owen is going to be a senior with me, captain of the varsity lacrosse team. It's not like I hang out with them, but I don't mind them, either, and lately they've been calling me Girl. As in, "Hey, what's up, Girl?" and "Girl, you're twisted smart," and "Girl, we're really sorry about what happened to your mother."

Now Old Olson is heading our way in his mint-colored converted golf cart—he'd gone upstream, to the bridge, crossed over, driven down. In the back are the shovels and buckets and sifters and picks for the coming excavation. "Miss Martine's been wanting herself a gazebo," he explains. "She has chosen this here as her perfect spot. Only problem is you'd have to airlift a bulldozer in, and that she has decided against. So we're hand digging—Miss Martine's special instructions. And we're hand digging until we are done."

"That woman is off her rocker," Owen says.

"She's the boss," Old Olson says. "She pays the bills."

Reny hitches up his pants with his thumbs, doesn't budge. Ida reaches down into the grass and pulls up a fat blade, begins tearing it into streamers. So it's me Old Olson starts to study, beneath his worn straw hat. "Step on up, Girl," he says, "and choose your weapon." I eye the golf cart, ignore it, walk straight toward Ida. I bend down, select a stone near Ida's feet. Stone's as big as a soup pot and heavy. I stagger once, then I stand straight. I'm not letting weakness show.

"Where do these go?" I ask Old Olson, cradling the thing in my hands.

He points past the fat tulip tree where Danny is posted, arm crossed over arm, every single muscle announcing its most beautiful self. "Past the resident workhorse," he says, tossing a toothy gleam in my direction.

"Girl's got muscles," Owen says as I make my way.

"You just going to stand there," Danny asks, "and watch her?"

"Nope," says Owen, and now he collects a stone, and now Ida and Reny and Danny are bending down and scooping, too, and now it's all of us taking the wall away from where the wall had been, so that we can get to the secret earth below. Specks of dust rise up, like pale, winged things. There is the smell of something ancient. A butterfly, a purple one, moves in and out of shadow.

Chapter Three

Tonight the master chef is making trout with saffron butter. He has an orange stain below the collar of his white work shirt and an apron tied around his waist, something floral that even Mom wouldn't wear because it is that wussy.

"New dish?" I ask.

"Prepare yourself," Dad says, "for the spectacular."

"You need a bib," I tell him, giving the hairy eyeball to his stain. "Not an apron."

"You need manners," he says.

He's cleared the paper from the kitchen table. His hair is a little less mad-scientist tonight. He's set three places like he always does, put a garden rose in a vase on the table. "Just in case," he once said, and I knew what he meant, I know that this, in addition to staying busy, is how he goes on surviving. He makes dinner an event, because that's what Mom did; it is his way of not letting her down. He says if Mom wants to show up as a guest sometime, he's damn well going to be ready. Tonight there is salad along with the trout and rolls he has warmed in the oven.

"We're doing a dig at Miss Martine's," I tell him as we sit down.

"To where?" He raises his eyebrows.

"To four feet deep, or something like that. Turns out she wants a gazebo."

"Odd. Thought she had one already."

"She wants two."

"Says who?"

"Says Old Olson."

"For what purpose?"

"He didn't mention."

"Didn't you want to know?"

"I didn't ask."

"Don't you find it strange? The perfect recluse, wanting a gazebo number two, and at her age?"

"Of course it's strange. But no stranger than you, hiding out with your paintings."

"Watch it now."

"Well, I'm just saying."

"You make me mad, and then what do you have?" He smiles through a long, fat pout.

"Peanut butter and jelly," I say.

"Peanut butter and jelly forever and ever."

I give him a look, so he knows I understand.

"No ragging on me about my solitude, okay? When's the last time you hung out with Jessie?"

"Well, anyway," I say, returning to my point, because I'm not getting into the old get-back-out-there-with-your-girlfriends conversation, "we're digging. It's just me, Ida, Reny, Danny, and Owen, and we've only got four weeks."

"You'll do it."

"Four feet," I complain.

"Think of it as archaeology."

"This isn't Egypt, Dad."

"You may be amazed by what you find."

He starts pushing his salad all over his plate, and I take a little taste of fish, and the truth is that it's not half bad, but Dad doesn't need me to tell him. "Well, if I do say so myself," he says, with that goofy smile on his face, and right then it hits me hard, a big whack from a blind angle: I wish Mom could see this. I wish she could see Dad with his saffron stains and his green apron and his rose-in-vase, trying to make things so right, trying to make like she isn't gone, like I won't be gone in a year. He still wears his wedding band on his wedding finger and the braid of leather around his wrist that Mom bought him in Barcelona. He still drinks blackberry lemonade in summer, Mom's favorite beverage. Suddenly I do not feel like talking.

The kitchen window goes from dusk to black. We finish, I clear the plates away, I scour and soap and wipe the counters down. "Good night, honey," Dad says, and he pushes back and walks away, goes down the long hall with the old things, and turns on the TV. It is three hours at least before Letterman. The kitchen is good and clean. I go out the back door and sit on the stoop, take a very good look at the moon. It has been hanging close all summer long. Tonight it is wide, and full with its craters and jags, and there is this halo that swirls around and keeps on going.

The moon throbs. There's only cricket song and nervous birds and Sammy Mack in the house across the street, screaming bloody murder at whoever is giving him a bath. Later I'll see him through the window, jumping from bed to bed in his room. Sammy needs a trampoline. And he needs a whole truckload of patience besides.

Do you ever wonder what a soul is made of? If it's moon dust or moonlight? "Mom?" I say, as if she can hear me. "Mom, you there? Anywhere?"

Chapter Four

The next day the finch is at it again, earlier this time, even louder. I prop myself up on both elbows and shake the bangs out of my face. The thing is bright as a canary with a hooded face, a lovely little devil, as my mother would have said. "You win," I tell it, but now it's hammering again, stopping only to cock its head before it revs back up. My room is a minty green except the window wall, which my mother painted white when I was born, and the windows are the old-fashioned kind with real, splintered-up mullions. Attacking one single, specific pane, the finch goes at it. Always the same pane, always the same exact spot, as if it is on its own excavation.

Beyond the finch is the top of the old maple tree. Beyond the tree is the sky and the sun. It's still the cranberry-ginger part of dawn. Not even Dad's coffee is on. What if the glass breaks and the bird flies in? What if the whole upstairs shatters and crumbles? I imagine the finch making a nest inside my lamp shade—dropping its feathers into my shoes, over my bedspread, over my pillow, over me. I imagine everything giving way to the finch. Suddenly I'm thinking about Miss Martine, who makes her desires known through good Old Olson. "Miss Martine has requested a lavender border," he'll report. "Miss Martine wants the narcissi deadheaded." "Miss Martine wants the black-eyed Susans thinned and a branch of Korean dogwood for the centerpiece of her table."

Once I looked her up in the local public library.

She was as stunning as Ida sometimes says—the only-child heiress on every bachelor's arm who never did get married. She was born April 8, 1938, which makes her sixty-nine years old, and it has been fifty-three years since she's last been seen in town, last thrown a party on her lawn, or been seen with any guy—rich or old or ugly. She's had her own kind of vanishing, and when I ask Ida why, or even Reny, they say the story goes that she stopped her socializing after a whopper of a storm blew straight through town. "Storm like a bowling ball," Reny says. "Tore the roof off a bunch of houses. Set a barn on fire. Ripped a train right off its tracks. Things died. People got frightened. That's what they say anyway, because I wasn't here; I was miles from here, doing my growing in the Blue Hills." Old Olson has known Miss Martine all his adult life. That is why, the rumor goes, he is trusted with her wishes.

Dad is up now; I can hear the coffee huffing. I tell the finch to go and knock itself out. I grab my stuff and go down the hall to the shower, past the door that my father keeps shut. My mother's things are in there——her clothes, her jewelry, her boxes of shoes, her collection of tinted glass bottles. She had lined up the bottles on every inch of windowsill, so that the room would never repeat itself——would be the color of whatever bottles the sun struck, whatever ways the reflections mixed on the walls and on the ceiling. "It's like being inside a giant kaleidoscope," she said. And the thought of that made her happy.

In the end, after the doctors said that there was nothing they could do, after my father had begged for a better answer, after I hated every living thing for living past my mother, the kaleidoscope was all my mother did——she watched the room change as the sun moved toward and then beyond her. There'd be spots of lilac and tangerine and moss green on the ceiling up above. There'd be shades of ruby in the creases of her pillow.

"You're so beautiful, Claire," my dad would tell her. But mostly he would sit there, saying nothing. The chair where he sat is still there, empty. The colors collide, but no one's watching.

Chapter *Five*

The dust has settled, but now there are bugs—a little blue-black cloud of them that, no matter what, won't swat away. I've tried my hand, I've tried my shovel, I have even tossed a rock, and Ida says, "Did you think that gardens were somehow bug-free?" and Owen says, "I don't think they're biting." Old Olson says that bugs are why we kids are paid more than the minimum wage, and shrugs and walks away.

They're too small to be mosquitoes, and they're definitely not flies, and even if they don't bite I hate the buzz-saw sound of them. After a while, Danny sighs and says, "Girl," then he reaches into his backpack and hauls out a Boston U cap. "Keep it," he says, plunking it onto my head. "I've got an extra at home." He pulls the bill down to my nose. He makes a little fan wave in front of my face, smiles his glossy white smile. Maybe it helps some, but I pretend it helps a lot and skulk back over to my edge of the hole. Everyone's been given a different side to dig. Reny's stuck with the part that has the fattest roots.

Yesterday evening Old Olson chalked the site, and this morning I picked out a shovel from his old golf cart and started wedging in. Where the wall had been, the earth was still moist; there were snail shells and grub backs and a knot of string and all the bacteria and fungi that I knew from school had to be there, but that I couldn't see. I could go maybe four inches in, and then the earth got different—hard and stubborn, like it was protecting something, and now every shovelful is a gigantic effort, and it hurts. I am the Girl, and I am the youngest, but no way am I the only one who is having a tough time, because even Danny's face is showing strain as he grips the shovel harder and puts more weight against the blade. The earth, four inches in, doesn't want to budge, at least not across the stream at Miss Martine's, and now Reny is complaining— swiping the sweat off his high brow and saying, "A gazebo? Really, Old Olson? Is this your idea of a joke?" Ida has big wet marks all over her white T-shirt. Owen has stopped for a bottle of Gatorade. I get a flash of my dad back home in the cool of his garage. I'd give anything to be there, giving him grief.

"Pickaxe would come in handy," Old Olson says after a while.

"Didn't fit in your cart?" Reny asks him.

"Left it up at the top of the hill, against the back

side of the main house. Was using it yesterday for a project."

"A knock-the-door-down project?" Ida asks Old Olson, and I don't know, I genuinely don't, why he puts up with her in the first place.

"I'll get it," I volunteer, before anyone else can.

"Get what?" Owen asks, because I guess he's been orbiting outer space somewhere with his Gatorade.

"The pickaxe."

"I can get it after lunch," says Old Olson.

"No, really," I say. "It isn't any problem," because truly it isn't, it's a blessing—I can go around and over and back down and come back to a hole that's more deeply dug. I can even outrun the bugs, or try. And at the end of it all, I'll have been helpful.

"Go on, then," Old Olson says. "Quick as you can."

"See Girl run," Owen says. I tug at Danny's cap, and I'm off.

* * *

I go the long way around because the slope's less steep, and because there's more shade that way. Walking Miss Martine's estate is like traveling around from country to country. She's got beds of red flowers, only red. She's got groves of apple trees, and apples only. She's got a pretty pebble garden that Yvonne weeds every morning, and everything that isn't pebbles is either orange or pink. You can move from one country to the other, though some countries are divided by stone walls like the stone wall we just moved; Reny claims that walls like these kept the herds of Ayrshire cows from straying.

High on the hill Amy's thick, dark hair tumbles out of her straw hat as she bends in next to Peter, who snips away at the bottom branches of some tree. Yvonne is higher still, alone, taking care of the gladioli and the dahlias. On the opposite side of the hilltop is Miss Martine's house—the same stone as the Ayrshire walls, a million tiny windows, a wide, three-sided porch, a big gray door that is the color of the massive slated roof. Where there are no shutters, there are curtains, and the curtains are always closed. There are pots of sweet Williams on the wooden railing of the porch. If you were just driving by, you wouldn't guess that anything was strange.

But the house smells ancient like the earth, damp like the day after a storm. There is silence; nothing moves; there are no cats sleeping in the shady parts and no dogs getting snippy. Miss Martine's is quiet as the stones down in the stream, quiet as the robin's nest that Danny found the other day, which had been lived in, then abandoned.

I don't dare knock, and I don't dare stand there staring. I hurry around to the back, to where the porch finally stops, and the pickaxe is there in a thin ray of sunlight, leaning against the house just as Old Olson had promised. I reach for it, and it is wood handled, heavy.

I bend a little in the knees, and as I pull it up toward me, I stagger back, stepping—I don't mean to—into a bed of pachysandra. I hear the snap of green things at my feet, the crunch of leaves that had more living in them, and suddenly I am certain I've been seen. I look up, and nothing moves. Only in the far right corner window of the second story does a white curtain dance in the breeze. Behind that curtain a shadow moves. Or nothing moves: I can't be certain.

"Sorry," I say, not nearly loud enough, about the pachysandra. "Didn't mean to." Cradling the pickaxe, I step out of the patch and away. I take cautious, even-if-she's-watching-I-won't-look-nervous steps. I turn the corner of the house and start to run. When I reach the crest of the hill, I'm sprinting—wondering if Miss Martine ever saw me in the first place, if she's up there right now watching, standing in a new window, following me with her eyes. I try to get a picture of her in my head, fix her—old and stooped, or tiny and light, her hair in a braid in a coil around her head, or her hair cropped close and neat. Who is she? I wonder. What has time done to her? But every time I've asked Ida to describe her, she won't; every time I've asked Reny, he grunts. I only have, in my head, an image of Miss Martine young, old-newspaper young—small boned, fit, dark haired, alluring, but not what my mom would have called delicate. Mom was always making distinctions like that. Find the fine line, she would say, and understand all that it separates. The fine line at Miss Martine's is between the living and the dead or dying, between all that is growing and all that has stopped behind the walls of the heiress's house. I am glad for Danny's cap and the shadow that it lays across my face. I am glad for the hill that falls down hard and fast.

"Long time coming," Ida says when she sees me making the leap across the stream, which isn't, by the way, an easy thing to do with a pickaxe in your arms. From the looks of things they haven't gotten too far;

the hole is much like it was.

"We thought you'd absconded," Reny says, pulling a long finger down one of the lines in his face.

"Hey," I say. "I've traveled miles."

"Give me that thing," Danny says, and I hand it over, gladly. He fits his hands around it like he's testing out a baseball bat. He digs his feet in and takes one impressive swing. The earth beneath the blade breaks up. There's a minicloud of dust. "Not bad," he says, and now Owen wants to take a turn, and there's another blast of dust. "This'll work," he says to nobody, and the two of them go at it now, two brothers with an axe. There are buckets in the back of Old Olson's cart. I get enough for the rest of us, so that we can haul the first layer of dirt away.

"Keep it up," Old Olson says when he's satisfied that we've got ourselves a system.

"Looking forward to the champagne," says Reny.

Chapter Six

D ad's got himself a new painting. It arrived today in a U-Haul truck, courtesy of some local museum that itself got the painting courtesy of some anonymous donor. He says that it came all mummy wrapped, not as tall as me, but more than twice as wide as I am tall. It's so messed up, he says, that you can only see dark shadows of things—figments, he calls them, that suggest a world.

"What kind of a world?" I ask, waiting for him to

finish his lemoned asparagus, which he eats with his fingers as if each stalk were a carrot stick.

"A metropolis," he says, raising his eyebrows and wiping his hand across his apron lap before reaching for a roll.

"Which metropolis?"

He's sprinkled capers on the veal, like olive-colored salt pills.

"None that I've ever seen." He slaps half a stick of butter on his warmed-up bread, which is something he and Mom would have fought about, except that they hardly ever fought. "At least I'll die happy," he'd say if she wrinkled her nose, but he'll never say that again, because happiness, we know this absolutely now, is not what dying is about.

"So this is it now? This painting? Your next big thing?"

"Biggest canvas I've ever worked on." He smiles. "A veritable mystery. It arrived at the museum wrapped in shower curtains. Polka-dotted shower curtains that had a crust of mildew."

"Weird," I say.

"Which reminds me," he says. "How is our Miss Martine?"

"Same as always."

"Another figment, wouldn't you agree?"

I nod and shrug at the same time. "I was up around her house today."

"Did you knock?"

"No way. You kidding?"

"I knocked once."

"You did?"

"Your mom sent me out with a basket of fruit. She'd heard it was Miss Martine's birthday."

"When was this?" I ask, and I'm about to say, And why did you never tell me?

"Your mother was pregnant with you at the time. She'd been talking to somebody who knew somebody who knew about Miss Martine's big day. She said that if nobody else was going to throw the heiress a party, she at least could send her some fruit."

"Except that she sent you."

"She did. That's true. Because she was pregnant and I insisted."

"So what happened?"

"Nothing happened. No one opened the door."

"Not even Old Olson?"

"Not even."

"That's strange."

"Figments," he says. "I'm telling you." He puts the last of the butter on his little shelf of roll, then wipes the leftover juices from his plate. He chews away and swallows down, then unties his apron. "I should go on one of those reality TV cooking shows," he says.

"Right."

"I should," he says. "I would be famous."

"I thought you already were."

"There's famous, and then there's famous. I'm thinking of going for the second kind."

"Sounds like you've got a painting to restore first."

"I've got a painting," he says, "to resolve." He looks at me, and I see the dark beneath his eyes.

"I'm on cleanup duty," I say.

"I'll trade you cleanup duty for a call you make to Ellen or to Jessie. I'll give you the car. I'll lift the curfew."

"Hey, but no thanks," I say.

"You sure, Katie?"

"I'm sure."

"You're a good kid, you know. You don't have to be a perfect one. I'm okay here, on my own."

"Will you get out of here?" I tell him, reaching to collect his plate. "You'll miss your show." He looks at me with his sad eyes and drinks down the rest of his lemonade.

* * *

The weird thing about cricket song is how the sound never stops but there's still space between the beats. On the front stoop I sit and think about this, try to picture the crickets in the grass, the way Mom once explained them to me. She said that crickets think in terms of trills and pulses, that they use their abdomens and their wings to sing, and that cricket singing is a big male thing; the females can't get a note in. "These guy crickets just sit around all day waiting for their chance to sing," she said, and I remember that she was brushing my hair, that we were sitting out on the stoop together, both of us in our summer pajamas; I might have been six, maybe seven. On the warmest nights, Mom said, crickets chirp the fastest, and tonight being warm, the songs are high and rapid, the songs are swelling everywhere and from all directions.

Through the door I hear the sound of the TV, the gusts of buggy laughter that have a rhythm all their own. Across the street I hear Mrs. Mack going after Sammy, begging him to climb down from the flat part of their roof. She uses logic and kindness before she starts promising treats, and then she gets into her desperations, her bleating, as Dad likes to say, and Sammy knows it, Sammy's king, and now Mrs. Mack is going to have to wait for her kid to get bored with her defeat. It'd be better for us all if Sammy's dad were home more.

Then again, Sammy isn't all bad, because he's dropped some gifts our way, not that he would know it, or understand the irony. It was because of Sammy that Mom said that we'd all had enough. That we had to get away last summer and not just for some weekend at the shore. I was lying on my bed with a book when she poked her face through my door. "Babe," she said, "I've had an idea. Let's go find your father." Her green eyes were full of light, the way they got when she was feeling certain. Her auburn hair was knotted back. Mom always wore skirts, even on nothing days. She had on a pair of rhinestone flip-flops.

Putting the book aside, I followed her down the long

hall, down the wide, curvy stairs, which drop beneath the photographs of my mom's family history, beneath the portraits—bright as candles—of her mother and her father. We cut out the side door and over the drive to the garage, where Dad was at work with the radio on, singing along with some old song. "To what do I owe," he said, looking up from his bottles, his brushes, the canvas, "the pleasure?" He snapped off the radio and removed his glasses.

Mom said, "Katie and I have some news."

"A conspiracy," he said.

I looked at Mom, because I still knew nothing, and because she was keeping us waiting, like she did— everything was a show with her, everything having to sparkle. "Barcelona," she announced finally. "I've already bought us the tickets." She threw her long skinny arm across my back and pulled me in tight against her.

"Barcelona?" I repeated, and the word echoed in the bigness of Dad's work space. "Barcelona?" I searched my head for something I might know, but in tenth-grade history we'd focused on the U.S. of A.

"When, honey?" Dad asked.

"Saturday," my mother answered. "And it's entirely unrefundable."

"But Claire," Dad said, glancing back at his canvas with a sudden look of panic. "Claire. Honey."

"It's all right, Jimmy. I called the Kazanjians. They're willing to wait an extra month. They're not even going to be around most of the summer."

"A *month*?" Dad said. "You've made arrangements for a month?"

"One complete Sammy Mack–free month," she said. "In the very heart of the Gothic quarter."

"When did this happen?" Dad asked, still more stunned than happy. "And how?"

"Google is my new best friend," Mom declared. Long strands of her hair had gotten loose from the clip. She shook it out, then bunched it up again. She walked between all the jars and brushes and things and planted a big kiss on Dad, his forehead first, and then his lips. All I was thinking was how little-girl she was, how she had lately seemed, at least to me, the youngest of us three.

"I've always wanted to see Barcelona," Dad said finally.

"Picasso," she said. "Gaudí. The Rambla." And the truth is that she was pale even then and her skirt fell loose, that if I had been smart enough, I would have known to worry, I would have guessed. But all I could see was the light in her eyes and the way Dad kissed her back and how the hair fell out of the clip again and it made her even prettier.

Sammy Mack was the excuse; that's all. She knew. Thinking back on it all tonight, I'm certain. Sitting here on this stoop I wonder if I'll ever be so brave as her, if she passed along her courage.

Chapter *Seven*

I wasn't hanging around for that head-banging bird; I just wasn't going there this morning. I got out of bed when it was still dark, went downstairs, tiptoed past Dad, threw some lunch into my backpack, stuffed a granola bar into my pocket. "See ya," I wrote on a note to Dad. "Have a blast." Then I was on my bike, and that's where I am now, smashing molecules with my silver zipper, breaking the atmosphere apart. It's all big estates between our house and Miss

Martine's. Even though it's August, the lawns are mostly green, the border flowers mostly on fire, and I can't hear if the cicadas are out; there's too much wind in my ears.

The road dips, banks, straightens, banks up, and now I'm pedaling hard against an upward slant, not smashing anything. I stand and lean over my handlebars. By the time I reach the two stone posts on either side of Miss Martine's drive, I'm completely out of breath, but here the angles work in my favor again, and I roll through, just like I always do, and start to zipper down again, rising near the house on the back of borrowed speed and sailing back down to the shed on the other side, where I park and chain my bike. Old Olson keeps some of the big machines here—the mowers, the whackers, the chain saws. The little minicart is gone, which means Old Olson is out there somewhere, and I go off toward the stream, sticking close to the dark ridge of shade. I stop behind the big birch tree and take a long look at the house. Some of the windows are on fire with the morning sun. The big old door is shut. Nothing emerges from the shadows. No one.

No Yvonne, no Amy, no Peter yet. Maybe not even Ida or Reny. It's an hour too soon for Danny and Owen, whose mother, power broker that she is, drops them off five minutes late each day, jabbering away on her cell phone. Beside stalks of blown-to-dust cattails I walk. Next to the windberry. Past something Yvonne calls prairie-drop seed that smells like black licorice.

At the edge of the watercress stream, by the crossing stones, I stop and make my way, looking for turtles and little green frogs and the snakes that make alphabet shapes. I'm quiet, and that's why Old Olson doesn't see me, doesn't even guess that someone's there, watching him watching the dirt that is the hole. He's squatted down to the ground, pitched out over the edge, sifting the soil with his hands, and I get a picture in my mind of the old gold miners in my history book, searching for their lucky strike. I can't imagine what's there, what Old Olson might be mining. If I ask him, I'll destroy the quiet. The nasty bugs haven't swarmed in yet, but there's a bunch of butterflies—monarchs with their stained-glass wings, twirling low and high. Old Olson, I think, is not as old as his name. His arms look strong beneath his shirt. His back is as broad as Owen's.

"Hey," I say finally, because it feels like spying, and just like that, Old Olson bolts up straight.

"You're early," he says when he turns to find me.

"Yeah, well," I say. "I guess." His eyes are truly very tiny, blacker than blue in this light. He doesn't seem all that glad to see me. "I've got this bird," I try to explain. "This bird that wakes me up."

"Parakeet?" he asks me.

"Finch," I say.

He looks at me as if I'm crazy. "Come back in an hour," he says. "With the others."

I take the backpack from my back and sling it up

against a tree. "Outa here," I say, and he watches me go; I feel his little eyes on me. I go back over the stones, to the stream's other side. I walk down and down, inside the shade. I don't turn to apologize or wave, I don't turn for a thing.

What just happened? I ask myself.

What is Old Olson hiding?

I take another long look back at the house and decide that it's wrong, it just is, that something as barren and sullen as that has been planted in a garden fat with color.

Chapter *Eight*

I take the long road back on my way home and stop midpoint at the library, which isn't as pretty a building as a library should be, but is huge and therefore full of something my dad calls capacity. Ms. McDermott glances up from the oak circulation desk, then gives me a longer-than-usual stare. "Sorry," I say, because clearly my dirtiness concerns her. "I already washed my hands. I swear."

Ms. McDermott is the coolest-looking librarian

ever—tall and thin, with straight highlighted hair and one of those noses you usually only see on magazine covers. When she puts on her glasses, it looks like she's doing an ad for fancy glasses. When she comes out from behind her desk, you get to see her magnificent shoes. But as stylish as she is, Ms. McDermott has never been married.

"What have you gotten yourself into, Katie D'Amore?" she asks in her low librarian voice, and I tell her that I'm spending the summer at Miss Martine's, working on the excavation team.

"It's for a gazebo," I explain, feeling less than lovely in my own muddy work boots and my borrowed Boston U cap.

"A gazebo," she repeats, and her nose crinkles. "And how can I help you with that?" Ms. McDermott is perpetually helping me. Even when the school library has the goods, I prefer to come here, for her brand of advice. Most of the kids from high school do.

"Research," I tell her. "I'm just trying to get a sense for the history of the place."

"The history of Miss Martine's?"

I nod.

"Well, it's not like there's a book on that," she says. "Or any encyclopedia entry."

"I once read a little," I tell her, "on microfilm. Local newspaper stories."

"Well, yes." And now I can see that Ms. McDermott is thinking, that she's forgotten for the moment about me being a filthy mess. Bringing Ms. McDermott a challenge is like doing public service. Nothing pleases her more. "Give me a minute," she says, and she goes back into the office that sits right behind her desk, an office with windows for walls so that now I watch her work, bringing big books down from triple-thick shelves and checking the computer. She stands with her hands on her hips for a few minutes, then writes down a few things. Now she opens the door and comes back out to the desk, and the eyes behind her glasses sparkle. Brown eyes full of light.

"We may be in luck," she tells me, "though I can't be sure." She gestures for me to follow her as she leaves her post and begins to walk toward the basement steps. "Julia," she says to the girl who is putting returned books on a shelf, "will you take over for a sec?" Julia nods, and Ms. McDermott keeps walking—a quick walk in high heels all the way down the carpeted steps. I feel a tingle of excitement.

Figments, Dad had said. Maybe. Or maybe something else.

"The story is this," Ms. McDermott says, halfway down the steps. "A few months ago we received an anonymous gift. Big boxes marked LOCAL LORE just sitting outside under the overhang when I came to work one morning. Julia and I took a preliminary look, and it seems to be all twentieth-century stuff. Diaries mostly, and newspaper clippings, little ribbons and awards, some plaques. The records of what I'd have to call an amateur historian. I just took a look at our computer log. Looks like there are references to Miss Martine in there."

"You're kidding," I say, and now the tingle is a prickle.

"I am not." Ms. McDermott laughs. "But here's the thing: We're understaffed this summer, Julia and I. We haven't taken much more than a cursory glance at this gift, and so far I can't report a rhyme or reason to it. It's as if someone tossed an attic's worth of papers into however many boxes were required, then drove it all here to us in the dark and disappeared before we could ask questions."

"I don't mind," I say.

"There are seven boxes, Katie."

"It's not like I have to get all my research done today."

"Here is what I'm thinking, then. I'll set you up

in a study room—we've got plenty of spare ones in summer. You come in when you can and come to circulation for a key, and you can do your investigating on your own. All I ask is that you leave the boxes neater than you find them. Organize as you go, if you would, by dates or by themes, whatever seems best, and when you're done, lock up, give us the key. Let us know if you stumble onto something big."

"I will," I promise. Ms. McDermott studies me for a moment, pulling her fingers through her hair. She balances on top of her fabulous shoes. Then she continues down the hall, stops at a door, turns the lock with the key that hangs from the ribbon around her neck. When she flips on the lights, I'm beside her. I see a room full of cartons, boxes, books that have escaped their bindings.

"You have just been introduced to the library's dirty laundry," she says.

She walks toward one long folding table, where the

seven boxes sit, each one marked, as promised, LOCAL LORE. "This is it," she says. "I'll have them transferred to a study room tomorrow. Bring your own paper. Use pencils only. Be careful, as you can never tell what treasures might be found."

"This is awesome," I say. "I mean, like, totally unexpected. Like I didn't really think that I would find *this* much."

"Remember something, Katie," Ms. McDermott cautions. "History is never absolute truth. It's parcels and string and suppositions. It's what you make of it."

"Okay."

"Miss Martine is a legend around here. Things have been rumored and whispered. But before she was a legend, she was just a girl, and after that, she was just a young woman. "

"I guess so."

"Don't come to any quick conclusions is what I'm

saying. Whatever you're searching for, don't be too quick to find it."

"Thank you, Ms. McDermott."

"Tomorrow," she says, "we'll be all set up for you."

"You know, Babe," Dad says when I finally walk in, an hour late at least, probably more, "you shouldn't keep your personal chef waiting. Did you know, for example, that roast beef cooks itself, even after you remove it from the oven?" Dad has his jewelry of many eyeglasses around his neck, his thickest pair high on his head. He's way overdue for a haircut. Dinner has been sliced, scooped, served. He has removed his apron.

"I didn't know."

"We've lost our pink center."

"I'm sorry, Dad."

"You've got a phone," he says. "You could have called."

"It won't happen again."

"I should hope not."

Sitting down to a meal all sweaty and muddy is not my idea of polite. But if I go upstairs to shower and change, I'll leave Dad waiting longer. Gingerly, I pull out my chair.

"Were you having tea with Miss Martine?" Dad asks.

"You're funny," I say. "Ha-ha."

"Or a date with one of those Santopolo boys?"

"Yup. Dressed like this. I'm such a turn-on."

"So where were you, then?"

"At the library, with Ms. McDermott."

"You stood me up for books?"

"That wasn't my objective."

"What were you thinking?"

I slice into the roast beef, pushing a portion into the pillow of mashed potatoes that Dad has made from scratch, judging from the looks of the counter behind him. "There was this weird thing that happened at the estate today. Something that went down with Old Olson."

Dad's face goes from angry to worried in an instant. "What was that?"

"It's just that—I don't know. This morning I was early, right? And I thought I'd just get working. But when I got to the excavation site, Old Olson was alone. He was at the edge of the hole we're digging, sifting for something with his hands, but that wasn't the thing that made me wonder. It was what happened afterward."

"Which was?"

"He turned and saw me, and he wasn't happy. He asked me to come back in an hour. Basically insisted on it."

"Didn't want your help?"

"Wanted me gone is more like it. Probably it's nothing, but still, I couldn't shake this feeling."

"What feeling?"

"Like he was hiding something."

"I see. And how does Ms. McDermott figure?"

"Research."

"Okay."

"Just a little investigating."

"What do you imagine that you'll learn from the past?"

"Something more about Miss Martine and her secret."

"Why are you so sure that she *has* a secret?"

"Well, I mean, isn't it obvious? Beautiful rich woman disappears and never so much as shows her face all these decades later?"

"You think you can find the truth in a library?"

"I think that I can try."

"You think it's any of your business?"

I nod.

"Why?"

"Everybody's story is a lesson," I say, quoting from Mr. Weisler at school. Mr. Weisler is a total pain-in-the-butt kind of American lit teacher, but still you remember what he says.

"It's summer," Dad says. "Give yourself a break."

I dig deeper into my mashed potatoes, take a bite of the green beans with their fancy almond slivers. I sigh and don't talk for a while. "Dad," I say finally, "this is one luscious dinner."

"Imagine it warm," he says.

Chapter *Nine*

It's a noisy business, cleaning the kitchen after my father has been cooking, especially on a mashed-potato night. It takes me longer than it sometimes does, and I can hardly stand my grimy self, the weight of my work boots, the stink of my T-shirt, the hot itch of the scalp beneath the hair beneath Danny's cap, which I never did take off. All I want is to stand in the shower and let the day fall away from me, and now I finish scrubbing the final pot and turn it upside down in the drying rack. When I turn off the sink water, there is no sound. No mumbo jumbo of TV, nothing that my dad is laughing at.

"Dad?" I say, and walk through the kitchen, down the hall, to where he sleeps, but it's dark in here, and no one is lying on the couch, a pillow folded up against his stomach.

"Dad?" I call, louder this time, and I realize that the whole downstairs is dark, that he isn't even in the house, can be only one other place. I open a side door, and sure enough, the lights are blaring across the drive, the old stables lit up like the inside of a train at night. I see him and then I don't see him as he walks around the room, the goggle-sized glasses on his face, a skinny something in his hand. Every now and then, he steps before the painting, which is propped up in the room's center, looking like it's floating. Gently, he brushes his tool against one small square of the canvas, then steps back, then leans in close, then trades his goggles for the pair of glasses on his head. Mom used to love to spy on Dad when he was thinking. "Just try to picture," she would say, "the whirligig inside his brain." I can't do that. I can't even try. He's tried to explain his work to me, but it's still a mystery.

It's pretty out here. The moon is less than it was last night, and there are thin shreddy clouds floating around in front of stars, leaving blanks in the constellations. The airwaves are busy with crickets and cicadas, and Sammy Mack, bless his monkey heart, is oddly, fabulously quiet. I keep standing here grubby, watching Dad across the drive, until finally I make my way toward him. "Hey" I say, as I open the door. "Disturbing the genius at work?"

"It's the strangest thing, Katie," he says, not moving his nose one inch from the canvas.

"What is?"

"Just . . . I've never seen anything like it."

"Like what?"

"Like what I think is going to be here when I start removing all the dirt."

"You said it was a metropolis."

"Yes. But nothing of this earth."

"What do you mean?"

"I'm thinking that what we have here is someone's idea of heaven. I'm thinking it's a glimpse of the eternal."

"Well," I say.

We both stand there not talking, just studying the painting, and I honest to goodness don't know how he can make any guess about it. The thing looks cloudy black to me; it seems ruined.

"I spent the day taking photographs of it," he says.

I nod.

"Tomorrow I'm going to remove the stretcher. It needs a new lining before I can start cleaning. The original canvas is like sandpaper."

"Sounds difficult," I say.

"Goes with the territory," he answers. "I'll wrap it up, lay it down on Mylar, start to peel—it just takes time."

"If you need any help . . ."

"That's okay. You've got your own work to do."

"I could help you at night," I offer.

"Thanks, honey," he says. "But you work too hard as it is already, and now you've taken on research."

"Tomorrow I won't be as late, Dad. I promise."

"Let's meet halfway on this," he says, "I'll push dinner back to seven, if I can count on you being on time."

"Deal," I tell him.

"All right, then," he says. "Now will you please go take a shower? That T-shirt is starting to reek and that cap doesn't do you one single ounce of justice."

"You're no peach yourself," I say. I leave him laughing.

* * *

The house is incredibly dark when I step back inside. I find the switch that lights the staircase and wind past the gallery of photographs—my grandmother, her mother, their border collies, the midnight-colored horse with the diamond of white stuck right in the middle of its forehead. There's a picture hanging here of my mom in a girly Easter dress, and that's my favorite photo, because Mom is already wild and not at all what rich girls were meant to be. She wears soft gloves but holds her shoes, and her feet are bare. She's laughing at something you can't see, and her hair falls in big, loose curls, tossed by the breeze. When I was younger, I used to carry this photograph all around the house with me. "Tell me a story," I'd say to Mom, and Dad would say, "Oh, don't get her started," though he didn't mean it, because he loved her stories. He'd stop whatever he was doing just to be there as she told them.

I hit another switch at the top of the stairs, and that lights the hall, which really looks more like the wing of some big, old inn, where they park room-service carts outside doors. The hardwood floors are scratched from my roller skating days. The wallpaper is from medieval times, or something pretty close. When Mom was alive and I was younger, our hide-and-seek went on for hours. She always won because she knew the places I hadn't yet discovered.

In Barcelona, she couldn't sleep. By day, we would walk from the old city to the new city all the way to this place they call Sagrada Família, which is a church that looks like a painted sand castle that they've been building for years but cannot finish, don't ask me why; even the tour guide couldn't explain it. We would stand in lines and we would walk through the church, around the construction, up into the towers, over and down, and then we'd walk all the way back to our hotel to rest, stopping at theaters or shops as we walked. She wanted to be by the sea at dusk—by the boats that bobbed on the back of the Mediterranean, and at midnight she wanted tapas, she wanted dancing, she wanted, but I only get it now, life. In the morning she'd be out of the room before Dad and I had awakened, just taking a walk, she would say, or buying oranges on the Rambla, or hunting down some pastries for our breakfast.

One afternoon I was up in the room reading my summer book for A.P. English when Mom pushed through the door. "You have to see this," she said, and she led me by the hand down the hall to the elevator and out onto the streets, then toward the square, where these musicians who had gathered before some government hall were banging and playing and calling. They had burned-bottom pots in their hands, big wooden ladles, teakettles, and also real instruments like brass trombones, harmonicas, accordions, and flutes. It was all just noise, not song, and some people were shouting over it, and I asked my mother what was going on, and she said, "I don't know, and I'm not sure it matters." She had so much light in her eyes, and what I kept thinking was, *So this is Barcelona. So this is my mother loving Europe.*

The sun was hot, but she stayed pale.

The days were long, but she wanted them longer.

There were mimes in Barcelona, I remember. They'd paint their faces white and their mouths grossly huge, then stand in the sun and stare at the crowds and not ever break their silence. "Imagine not speaking like that, for hours and hours," Mom would say. The thought of it making her shudder, but I didn't understand why.

"Mom?" I call out, because I hate the silence of this house. "Mom?" Her door is shut and I lean hard against it, and then I walk a couple of doors farther and deliver myself to the shower.

Chapter Ten

The next day I get to Miss Martine's early, but this time I don't let on that I am here. I stand back instead, watch from the other side of the stream, and wait for Old Olson to show up in his mini-cart, to rumble on in from the other side. He does after a while, after some of the early-bird bugs have started buzzing—parks his machine under the umbrella of a tree, climbs out, and walks (and I knew he'd do this) directly to the hole, which we pickaxed and shoveled out yesterday until we hit a smooth minus two feet all around. Reny says we might as well be shoveling dry concrete, and yesterday Owen, red and real hot, tossed the axe to one side and pounded the pit with his fists. "You're looking ridiculous," Danny leaned in and told him, but it was Ida who snapped him back to his senses. "You've got a girl watching, young man," she said. "And I do not believe you are making an impression." Owen looked up and Danny offered a hand. Then Owen climbed out on his own. He swiped the dirt from his knees, picked up the axe, and we finished the day without much talking, except for saying, over and over again, that it was much too hot. Through it all Old Olson kept his station by the tree—looking on but not pitching in, which is your choice, I guess, when you're the boss.

Now Old Olson squats down and balances himself with one hand. With the free one he starts digging around, raking his fingers through the crumbles of dirt, same kind of action as yesterday's, until I went and scared him. Whatever he wants he hasn't yet found, and now he's raking with the other hand, but again he comes up empty, and he stands, removes his hat, scratches hard at his bright white snow-colored hair. Tall as he is, with his white hair shining, I suddenly wonder why he works at an estate at all, why he keeps himself hidden beneath a hat. Mom would have said that he has a quality to him. Something stand-outish, when he's not in disguise.

Hearing something, I turn, take my eyes off Old Olson, see Ida and Reny cresting over the top of the hill. She moves like a wall with legs, swings her right side forward and then her left side forward, while Reny is more like a flamingo. The widest parts of his legs are his knees, which pluck up and down like someone's yanking at knee-maneuvering strings. Ida has to take four steps to keep up with Reny's two. They've seen me. There's no sneaking out of view.

"Hey." I wave to them, and me calling out makes Old Olson turn. "Morning, Old Olson." I wave to him, too.

"Early again?" he calls out, across the watercress stream.

"Just got here."

"Well," he says, giving me a long look with his little eyes, "we might as well get started." He puts his hat back on, and I stone-to-stone it across the stream, toss my backpack, walk to the cart, pick up a flat-faced, steel-handled shovel. I whack it down at the hole, and soil scatters. I whack it down again and collect the loosened dirt with the blade of the shovel.

"Girl's got the knack," Reny says, and Ida gives him the shut-up eyeball.

It's a little after that when Danny and Owen show up and take their places—Danny moving quicker than Owen down the hill, and apologizing for both of them. "If I had a car," Danny grumbles, "this being late would never happen." Owen gives him a look like "Yeah, speak for yourself," and Old Olson keeps his arms knotted as he leans against a tree. Butterflies do their gliding thing and scatter. The bugs buzz. Reny starts to whistle "She'll Be Comin' 'Round the Mountain," and Ida hums like she forgets that there are others of us here. You don't talk much when you work like this. You don't let Danny see that you're watching him, or Old Olson know that you're suspicious. And you don't ask Ida and Reny the questions you've got about Miss Martine at the top of the hill.

At break, I join Danny and Owen on the other side of the stream, where they've spread out their stuff beneath the trees. I yank my napkin from the backpack, pull out yogurt, a ripe peach, a Ziploc bag of smashed-up crackers. I blow some air into the sticky mess of my long bangs, which have gotten stuck beneath Danny's cap. The Santopolos both have hoagies, the stuffed-full, foot-long kind, and no one says anything until we're mostly through with our lunch, when Danny squeezes his fist into his khakis pocket.

"Dude," Owen says, when Danny uncurls his fingers. Owen has four inches at least of his hoagie left, and a golden glow of mustard on his lip. Putting down the hoagie, he smears his mouth with his fist, which leaves a trace of dirt beneath his nose. I'd give him grief, except that I'm too busy staring at the thing on Danny's palm. "What *is* that?" I ask, because it's half a hand long and half a finger skinny and also pale and knobbed and Swiss cheesy but hard. It seems snapped at one end; it's a fraction.

"Can't say that I know for sure," Danny says. Owen sweeps it right off Danny's hand and lifts it up toward the light. "But you ask me to guess, and I'd guess bone."

"Where'd you get it?" Owen asks.

"Where do you think? In the hole."

"Are there any more where that came from?"

"Do you think I know?"

"Well, you picked up this one without saying a thing. Who knows what else you saw and stole."

"You're crazy," Danny says. "I'm no thief."

I take the bone out of Owen's hand and glance past the guys to across the stream, where Ida and Reny are sitting—Ida with her legs kicked out, Reny with his chin resting on the table of his knees. Old Olson is nearby on his walkie-talkie. The three of them for sure aren't watching the three of us; we're just the summer help, while they're the real caretakers. I twirl the bone between my fingers. I touch the broken end. "Probably a cat," I say. "Or a raccoon. Don't you think?"

"Why not a horse," Owen says, "or a cow?"

"Owen," Danny says, "it's not that big."

"Big things have little bones too, you know."

"Biology is not your specialty."

"Whatever it is," I say, "it's got to be old, sitting

underground for all these years."

"I could use it for my culminating project," Owen says.

"Dude," Danny says, "you haven't started that one yet?"

"I still have most of this month."

"You've had three years for your culminating project. And no, you're not using my bone for your project."

"You're selfish, man."

"More like you're lazy."

"Whatever."

"Guys," I say, "chill out. Can't you? There are probably more where this came from."

"Ashes to ashes," Danny says, taking the bone back, burying it deep in his pocket, pulling his T-shirt up over his killer abs to wipe the sweat off his face. Owen picks up the rest of his hoagie and takes a whopper-sized bite. I spot a ladybug on a long blade of grass and give her a ride on my finger, and she takes her time. She goes up to my knuckle and zigzags back down, as if she has all day long to choose a direction, to live in this green garden with tree stumps, crumbles of seeds, bones—a cat, I'm sure it was a cat, maybe a tabby or a calico that belonged to someone who also, maybe on a bright day when things were blooming and ladybugs were swarming, disappeared. Vanished. Things disappear and vanish. That's the fact. Before you're ready for them to go, they go, and after that all you can do is keep the idea of them bright inside yourself. I place my finger alongside a blade of grass. The bright red dot climbs off.

"Hey," Owen says.

I look up. "What?"

"You think Miss Martine is really up there, in the house?"

"I don't know," I say. "Why do you ask?"

He shrugs. "I don't know. The bone. I thought . . ."

"That bone belonged to a cat, Owen. Seriously."

"It'd be more interesting," he says, "if it hadn't."

"Dream on," I tell him.

"Hey. It's a dig. Give it some credit." He smiles ridiculously, and I've got to give him props. Better to hope for something interesting with this work than to assume that it's as flat-out muscle-busting, mind-gnawing tedious as it is.

"Break's over," I say, glancing back toward Ida and Reny, who have pulled each other to their feet and are stomping about in their boots, rubbing their legs, to get the circulation going. Owen looks now, too, and laughs.

"We could use better partners in crime," he says.

"What we could use," Danny says, "is some rain."

Chapter Eleven

Past the drive, the road falls down so fast it feels like bungee jumping. A scrap of air gets caught between me and my backpack, tilts me back for half a second, and then is whooshed away, and I'm flying forward, both hands wrapped around the handlebars and the bangs beneath my cap blowing wild across my face. There are big puffs of shade on one side and yellow heat on the other, as if the clouds and the sun have all sunk straight into the ground. The cool side of the street is Miss Martine's side, until the fence that separates her from The Willows, which is the park with the goose pond where everybody goes in winter to make out or ice-skate.

Right about here is where I turn left onto a long, flat, straight road that is all shade on both sides at this time of day, except for where they're putting in a ring of new houses. This is my favorite road of all the roads I ever travel on, and it was Mom's favorite, too, which I know because she'd drive here and park and say floaty things like "Red really is the best color for a barn" and "What do you suppose they hide in silos?" Corn still grows along parts of this road, and the best houses are the old ones, real and solid and not trying for awards.

I slow down and take it in until the next crossroad, and here I hang a left. This road has houses at its start, then a house made into a bank, then the original post office, then a gravel parking lot, next to which is the library. The library has wide columns out in front and thirteen stairs you have to climb to get all the way up. The glass doors are plastered over with a zillion book club signs. You swing them open into a whopping AC blast. I get a real quick case of the chills, then my goose bumps settle down.

"Well, if it isn't Miss Katie D'Amore," Ms. McDermott says.

Too out of breath to speak, I finger my bangs back into place, adjust my backpack.

"Your room awaits you," she says. She unlatches the little half door at the circulation desk and starts making for the stairs, and I follow behind, thinking of just how fabulous she looks in her yellow tank top and white linen pants and spike-heeled hot-pink shoes. I don't even know how she can walk in those things, but she's a runway-quality walker. She must have studied fashion when she was majoring in books, must have modeled on the side; I'd bet on that.

At the bottom of the stairs we turn left, where the small rooms look like the interrogation rooms you see on TV detective shows. Ms. McDermott slips a key into the first door lock, snaps on the light, and there they are: the seven boxes of Local Lore. I have a fresh pad of paper in my backpack, a bunch of rubber banded number twos.

"You need anything," she says, "you ask me. I'm here till five today."

All I can say is "Thank you."

When she's gone, I take my seat at the long wood table and drag the nearest box into place. I pop the lid and now stand again, so that I can get a good look inside. It's like paper soup—photos and clippings, notes, an almanac, an odd-shaped leather binder. I reach for the binder first, which seems most promising. I lay it down, open it up to photographs—square and black-and-white, with jagged edges, a couple still stuck in their original places on the thick black paper, most of them detached.

With white pencil somebody has written words below where the photos are all meant to be. *Winter 1948. Honeysuckle season. Pooch takes a carriage ride. Croquet on the lawn. Lazy Sunday.* The photos are so small, blurred, and faded that I have to scrunch my eyes to bring them into focus, and even scrunched up my eyes are confused. It's hard to make out how what is now was what was then, because the roads are thin and the cars are funky and there are tons more trees and fewer fences. I sift looking for something familiar, and that's when I find the two entrance posts at Miss Martine's. They're squat and stone, just like they are in present time, but in the photo they're gobbed all around with flowers. At the very edge of the picture is the nose of a collie, but nowhere anywhere is Miss Martine. Not as a baby, not as a little girl.

Closing the book, I dip my hands back into the paper soup—start fishing stuff up at random. It looks like a tea bag was dragged across the old society news, and I'm worried that if I flatten the folds, I'll crack the history in two. I see a third of an ad for new country houses. A fraction of a story about a fox chase. A headline about a horse that has broken through its barn. The scores of a doubles tennis match. Then there is a cutout that looks a bit more interesting, and I shake it loose, extremely careful. The dateline reads November 15, 1953. Four paragraphs in, I find her.

Of course, the truest highlight of the evening was the debut of Miss Martine Everlast, only child of John Butler Everlast, chief executive officer of Quality Chemicals, and his wife, the former Andrea Bell. Not since Lillian Penwick has the Philadelphia Assembly Ball been graced by such transcendent lambency. Her silver peplum and chinchilla stole sent a shiver through the hall. A single pink diamond set off the midnight of her hair. She arrived with a bouquet of golden fleurs-de-lis.

"So here you are," I say, reading the paragraph several times through, closing my eyes, imagining an evening when Miss Martine was not much younger than I am now and turning the high-society heads at the Bellevue. "Transcendent lambency," *lambent* being a word from my SATs, something about gleam or flame or glow, and I picture a whole room of rich people stopping to admire her, bow their heads to her, raise their glasses, and how do you go from being a star to being a black hole? How do you end up hiding behind windows, if indeed she's hiding behind windows?

My mind catches on the fleurs-de-lis, and I remember a story my mother told, about a French king, fifteen hundred years ago, who had been trapped, with his men, by German Goths. There they were, stuck at the River Rhine, my mother said, and there were these fleurs-de-lis, rising from the river's center. Wherever the flowers rose, the river, the king knew, was shallow, and where there was shallowness, there was escape.

"The flowers were his guide," my mother said. "They saved his life." I picture Miss Martine with a diamond in her hair and the bright golden flags in her arms. Flowers as lifesavers, I think. Or as escape? What does it mean?

It's enough for one day. Enough to wonder through, and besides, I promised Dad that I'd be home for dinner and I'm not going to disappoint him. I layer everything back into the box, flip off the light, clomp up the stairs, tell Ms. McDermott that I'm done.

"Any luck?" she asks.

"Fleurs-de-lis," I answer.

"Fleurs-de-lis?" She looks quizzical at first, then smiles. "We call them flags around here, or irises."

"Yes," I say. "My mother explained it once. It's not much, but it's what I've got so far. I'm not counting on this to be easy."

"Katie D'Amore," says Ms. McDermott. "What fun is there in easy?"

Chapter Twelve

anny got what he was hoping for, which was rain, though this rain is like bright white sheets of fire, a genuine storm. It sounds like a thousand Sammy Macks dancing on the roof, and if I didn't know better I would say we're a big boat going down. The whole upstairs is an echo. There's the *drip-drip* of rain leaking somewhere inside. Even when I pull the sheets over my head, I can see the lightning. It was quiet out there when I went to bed. Now it's the end of the world, and the only good thing that I can think of is that there won't be work tomorrow.

The clock says two thirteen A.M., except that it feels like ten hours since I last checked it, like nothing is moving forward and day will never come. Sometimes when I close my eyes, I see Old Olson's hard blue stare and all the windows in Miss Martine's house in their impenetrable glare. I think of what Reny said, about the heiress disappearing on a night that might have been just like this one: September 10, 1954. A bowling ball of a storm, those were his words, tearing straight through, ripping up houses, leaving people frightened.

Two twenty-two. If this lasts any longer, we're all going to sink and get buried, too, in dirt so hard that they'll need to pickaxe through. I'm thinking it's the second guest room where the rain has broken through, and that I might as well get up and get the bucket that sits beneath the sink in my bathroom. I turn on my lamp first, then flip my wall switch. I feel along the hall, hit that switch, too, and all the way down to the bathroom, I drag my hand across the wall, like there's some kind of safety in that. I flood the bathroom with all its light when I get there, find the bucket and the biggest towel, and head back down the hall, push against the half-open guest-room door. The rain comes in through a crack in the window, splashes on the sill, on the floor. I push the bucket into place and use the towel to swipe and sop. In daylight I'll take a better look. For now this will have to do.

It is only after I've done as much as I can think to do that I notice the light across the drive. I blow on the window and rub away the steam, and if it's hard to see with all the rain streaming down, I'm not doubting that it's Dad. He's out there again, forgetting all about the time, not even remembering that he's missed another Letterman Top Ten. Probably he's not realized that there's a pour-down rainstorm yet, that there's firecracker lightning all around.

"Mom," I say, because if she were here, she'd have gone to get him, she'd have dragged him right back into the house, thrown a towel at his head, tossed him a pair of dry pajamas. Mom lost friends because she loved Dad, that's what she told me once, and I said, "Why, because he's crazy?" And she said, "No, because he has genius." She said that she knew from the first that he was better than brilliant, that he proved it to her though he wasn't even trying, when her parents both went down in a plane. She was twenty-eight when she brought Dad her parents' portraits. Four months later he'd brought their faces back to life. Mom was twenty-nine when Dad moved in, a few months short of thirty when I was born. I'll be going to college next year. I don't know what he'll do when I am gone.

Who could sleep with all this storm? I leave the window, go down the hall and the wide turn of stairs, cut out across the driveway. The rain falls hard as a full-blast spigot, spouts a river through my hair, smacks my T-shirt and my shorts against my skin; and I wish that I'd remembered shoes. I slam my weight against the door, flick a chip of gravel from my foot. Dad looks up, confused.

"What in the world?" he asks, as I stand there wringing the wetness out of me, turning the floor into a pool.

"Dad," I stare back, an exaggerated stare. "Do you know what time it is?"

He checks his watch. "Well, now I do."

"You have to sleep, Dad, you know."

"I'll get around to it."

"No. Really. I mean it. You have to take care of yourself. You would if Mom were here."

He winces, looks away, but lets it go. "Is my favorite pot calling the kettle black?"

"I *was* asleep," I say. "I was awakened by the storm."

"Same destination, different journey," he says. "You shouldn't worry so much about me." He pulls an old, clean towel from a cupboard he built and brings it over my way. Flaps it open and fits it like a shawl around my head. Gives me a kiss on the cheek.

"Upstairs window is leaking," I tell him.

"Your room?"

"Guest room."

"I'll get to it tomorrow."

He walks back over to the painting and stands before it. "You want to see something, Katie?"

"What's that?" I follow his trail.

"I was removing the stretcher, peeling the lining, and look what I happened to find." He's got some crumpled sheets of something in his hands. I have no idea what they are or what they mean. "Notes," he says, when I shrug and shake my head. "Notes the artist made about the painting."

"Well, that's cool," I say, distracted by the blast of

lightning that just ripped open the sky.

"Yes, it is cool," he says. "Turns out this was no ordinary painter."

"What do you mean?"

"Looks like John Butler Everlast had himself a little hobby."

"Are you kidding me?" I say, and I shiver a little, get goose-bumpy arms, and not because of the rain.

"These are his notes, and this is his painting," Dad says, and his eyebrows rise so extremely high that they're lost beneath his fringy hair.

"Well," I say. "I mean, like, oh my God. Are you kidding me? Are you serious?" Dad looks at me and laughs.

"Thing is," Dad says, "the notes are mostly in code. Chemical symbols, bits of shorthand. The guy was talking to himself."

"Or hiding something," I say.

"Or trying to figure something out."

"Or both."

"You know"—Dad sighs—"Mom would have loved this."

"Loved what?"

"The riddle," he says. "She'd have conducted a vigil right here until she figured the whole thing out." I close my eyes so that I can conjure Mom, and I don't open them for a while. When I look up, I see that Dad is lost behind his thickest spectacles.

Chapter Thirteen

The rain isn't going to stop. There's no sure line between darkness and dawn, and for all I know Dad slept on the studio floor or never slept at all once I came back to bed. The rain patter down the hall has slowed to a faucet-quality drip. I lie in my bed counting the drips, losing count, conjuring Mom, losing Mom, half dreaming, half expecting that bird. And then my dream turns into something else, and in my mind's eye, I am seeing Miss Martine with her fleurs-de-lis in 1953. All dressed up for a party.

What happened to Miss Martine with the pink diamond in her hair and the fleurs-de-lis in her arms? Why does Old Olson have us digging? I need to get back to the library today; I'll ask Dad for his car, and he'll say yes, but first I need at least two aspirin to fix the pain in my head. I hold my face with both hands as I climb out of bed. I take slow, extremely timid steps. I hear the languid drip from all the way down the hall, but now there is another kind of sound—this strange disorder behind the one locked door, the fluttering sound that birds make when they leave a treetop for the sky. It's a rushing toward and a rushing away, and then a sudden silence. I stand for a long time perfectly still, but whatever it was is gone now.

I take the long way to the library—loop around through my four-cornered town, past the drugstore, the bank, the theater, the ice-cream store and the sweet boutique, Pie in the Sky and Bread Basket. Then I swing a right into the old neighborhood, where the houses seem huge sitting up on their hills, surrounded by trees and soaked gardens. People say this place was built one hundred years ago by a crowd of Italian masons, and through the blur of the windshield it disappears, then comes back into view, vanishes and returns, the houses and the history are there, and now they aren't. It's so green back here, so big and unperturbed, and I drive without the radio on, so that all I hear is the click and slosh of the rain and the wipers and the rain, and all I can do is remember the days my mom and I would go walking out here, she holding my hand, she pretending that we could have any house, any hill, any tree we might choose. "Just imagine," she'd say, as if we'd gone shopping for shoes, and when she found something she really loved—a big, round room, a wraparound porch, a copper-finished turret—she'd stop on the sidewalk and stand, looking, saying, "Beauty endures, Katie. You try and remember that."

Back out on one of the winding roads I head toward the fox-chase grounds, which they're cutting up and ruining now with butt-ugly developer houses. All this is fenced-in land, sliced into parcels, and on some parcels the new, half-finished houses stand wrapped up in their Tyvek, and in some places there are machine-dug holes, and in others the weeds are growing all over the place, waiting for some millionaire's deposit. A little farther down there's a soggy stretch by a stream, which is still farmer owned and cattle grazed, and after that lie the Geringer Stables, where for four generations the finest Hanoverians have been bred and where, in a fenced-in area behind, little kids get their first rides on horses. Olympic horses, my mother always said, though most actually show at the Devon Horse Show, held once a year every May. Like the soggy cattle land beside it, Geringer Stables defies the developers. It's still standing and not going anywhere, though today, with the rain, it looks nearly abandoned. A couple of pickup trucks in the drive. Big cubes of hay stuck in rivers of mud. Somewhere back there Hanoverians wait for the sun to shine again, and somewhere back at her own estate, Miss Martine waits, too. Remembering what? I want to know. Watching for what through the rain?

There are only four other cars in the library lot, and I'm soaked through by the time I'm up the steps and through the door. I let my hair fall loose out of Danny's cap and fix my bangs with my fingers. "Morning," I say to Ms. McDermott, who is stamping date-due cards with that gunshot-sounding machine.

"Vacation day?" she asks.

"Weather related," I say.

She pulls open a drawer and draws out a key. "For you," she says. "Good luck."

I take my time going down, moving at slow-mo

speed. In the study room, I buzz the lights on, and they go *briitttt-britttt*, like a mosquito zapper. The boxes are just precisely as I left them. I choose LOCAL LORE box number two—slide it across the table. Then I lift the lid on more paper soup, but this time it's almost entirely newsprint, everything folded in quarters. Looks like the same old someone did overtime with the tea bag.

Monster patience. Research demands it.

Bit by bit, then, I flatten quarters into wholes and slowly turn the pages. The past is here, and most of it doesn't make a difference. Gentlemen's agreements, a face-lift for the local theater, a Fourth of a July parade. The photographs are yellow, grainy. I read the captions. By lunchtime I'm feeling dizzy. I lay my head down on the table and close my eyes to rest.

Two hours later I'm startled awake by a tapping noise, and for the first thirty seconds I think that the finch has found me here. I scrape my face off the table, turn, see Danny standing on the other side of the glass door. Chances are horrifyingly high that I have drool spilling down one corner of my mouth and that half my face is a pancake. "God," I say. "Danny. What are you doing here?" He's got a goofy grin, a tease in his eyes, and I am never going to hear the end of this.

"Ms. McDermott mentioned that you were down here," he says. "I thought I'd stop by for a visit."

"How did I come up?"

"I think I called the place a ghost town. She said, 'No, not really,' and identified you as another nonghost."

"Well, what are you doing at the *library*?" I ask, and I realize that it sounds like I'm accusing him of trespassing, as if this place were all my own.

"I read too, you know," he says, and now he crosses his arms and leans into the doorway, and I have to admit that when you take away the mud and sweat, Danny Santopolo is a not-half-bad-looking guy. "What about you?"

"Research," I mumble. I start massaging my cheek with my right hand, trying to erase the table tattoo I'm sure is there. My hair must look like a wet dog's coat—ruined by rain, smashed by a nap.

"Local Lore?" Looking past me, he reads the boxes.

"Miss Martine," I finally confess. "Just doing some digging."

"Digging? That's a good one." He smiles, and I feel my face grow hot, and when that happens I blush harder. Danny stands there just watching me. "Owen's still ticked off about the bone, by the way," he says at last. "Says he's telling Old Olson that I stole it unless I hand it over to him."

"I'm thinking there's more where that came from," I tell him. "I mean, maybe not bones, but something more than dirt and bug shells."

"Yeah. I'm thinking so, too."

I look into his eyes and decide that he isn't messing with me. "Why is that?" I ask, realizing, all of a sudden, that his eyelashes aren't all the same color. Some are lemon like his hair. Some are dark as his eye-brows.

"You ever drive past Miss Martine's at night?" he says. "Only ever the same light on, in the same exact room, always."

"Never noticed."

"Somehow doesn't strike me as an heiress with a gazebo on her mind. I asked my mom last night if she has ever even seen Miss Martine. She thought about it for half a sec before she told me no."

"I'm not onto anything yet," I tell Danny. "I mean, these are just some boxes. And I don't even know why I care so much, except that I just do. I can't see sitting like she does in one house all those years. I can't under-stand it." I don't tell him the other half: that if I can solve the mystery of Miss Martine, maybe I can also solve the disappearing of my mom. Maybe I can get to the heart of fine lines and survival.

"You need some help?"

He smiles, and I don't need convincing.

"Sure," I say, and he heads down the hall, comes back a few minutes later with his own metal library chair, sets it down beside mine. Sits, and we're so close together that our elbows are touching.

"So where are we?" he asks.

"Newspaper clippings," I tell him. "Just looking for her name in any story. Her name, also her father's." I slide some of the fished-out batch over his way. He smoothes the papers flat with his hand.

"The magnate, you mean."

"John Butler Everlast," I nod.

"Imagine living your whole life with a stuck-up name like that." Danny pinches his mouth together, turns up his nose, shakes the curls out of his face. "How do you do?" he says, bowing close.

"Pleasure's all mine," I say.

Chapter *Fourteen*

"Look who has come for a visit," Dad says when I find him much later in his studio. The rain has stopped, but the sky's still dark. Every studio lamp is blazing.

"Sammy?" I say, because there's no mistaking Sammy and his hair, which looks like one more fire burning.

"My new first-rate assistant."

Dad, I want to say, are you *serious*? *Monkey*? But

I hold my tongue and take a quick visual check, and this is the weird thing: Nothing's broken. Here Sammy stands in this room of glasses, jars, solutions, and resins, and there is no apparent damage, no aftermath of Hurricane Mack, no puddling paints, no drips. I look at Dad, and I know Dad knows precisely what I'm thinking. I look at Sammy, and he stands there staring—head cocked, fists punched into his sides, as if I'm the one intruding.

"Sammy's mom is attending to some business," Dad explains, making the arrangement sound official. "Baby-sitter canceled, and I said I could use the help."

"You were the next best thing?"

"I am *the* best thing. Don't you forget it."

"Lucky for Sammy," I say.

"Lucky for me," Dad says. "Look at how far we got. The canvas is almost back on its stretcher." Dad steps aside, and he isn't lying. The painting's beside him, all in one piece, with a spanking, brand-new liner.

"I helped," Sammy says now, flopping his head to the opposite shoulder.

"I see," I said.

"It was super easy."

"I bet."

"I have superhero powers." Now Sammy squats and grunts and points and hops and then he stands up straight. "I'm speedier than Spider-Man," he says. "Than Human Torch, even." He squats and groans and points again. His jeans are so loose that it looks as if he'll run right out of them. His T is two sizes too small. The red lights on his yellow sneakers flash.

"What's that you've got there?" I point to the little movable table beside him, and its jars and paints and brushes.

"I'm making my own picture," he says. "See?" He lifts a sheet of construction paper from the center of his table, and his colors start to drip down the page. Everything is either yellow or orange, and there are lots of jagged edges.

"Stars?" I guess.

"Rocket ships," he says, thrusting out his bottom lip, then forgetting his disappointment in the next half second as he plops down on a little wheeled stool to finish his creation.

"I think he's got talent," Dad says. "Don't you, Katie?"

"Uh, right. Sure."

"You remember when you used to paint out here?" Dad continues. "You were always painting flowers." I get a sudden flash of another me, sitting right near Dad, painting like Sammy. I remember Dad stringing a clothesline and pinning my paintings and calling to Mom, "Come and see Katie's show." Whatever Mom was doing, she would stop to praise me, always pick out a favorite. The favorites got hung on the refrigerator door, with the banana magnets. "How did the research go today?" Dad asks me.

"Okay, I guess. Nothing special. Tell you later."

Because who knows what Sammy might report back to his mother, and how can you keep a mystery a mystery if the whole neighborhood is in on it?

"I was thinking pizza for dinner," Dad says.

"Pizza?" I say. "Really? The master chef wants pizza?"

"Pepperoni, pepperoni, pepperoni," Sammy says, supposing, I suppose, that someone asked him. He holds his wooden-handled paintbrush up, as if he could paint the air, and stomps his feet so that his sneakers send up flares.

"I'm not eating pepperoni," I say.

"We'll do half and half," Dad says.

"Whatever," I say, turning for the door.

"Katie," he calls after me, "would you mind calling for delivery?"

Later Dad asks if I can walk the kid home, and what am I going to say: "No, I'm busy?" I moisten a wad of paper towels and wash Sammy's face. Then I pick him up all screaming and kicking and carry him to the sink and stick both his fists beneath the spigot. "Water's too hot," he complains, and I cool it down a bit. Then I dry him off and turn him around, and Dad says, "You're looking spick-and-span."

"Superheroes don't wash up." Sammy pouts.

"They do after pepperoni pizza," Dad tells him. Sammy looks at Dad like Dad might just be onto something. He stomps his flashing shoes toward the kitchen table and gives Dad a friendly upper-arm flick.

"I'm coming back tomorrow," Sammy announces.

"Are you now?" Dad says.

"Yeah, 'cause you need me," Sammy says.

"Well, we'll have to ask your mother."

I give Dad the are-you-kidding-me? stare, but Dad won't catch my eye. He runs his fingers through his lion's mane and slouches back against his chair. "See you, Sammy," Dad says. "Thanks for stopping by."

In the dark I reach for Sammy's hand. Without a fuss he gives it up. Wraps his fingers around my one finger so tight that I swear he's popped my knuckle. The clouds have all gone off somewhere, and the night is clear, and the crickets are going crazy, and there's *hoo-hoo*ing that could be an owl, could be a pair of mourning doves. Sammy's shoes light our way down the drive, until right near the end, where the big bulb in the old lamppost throws out a shine, and right there, in that shine, are the four glass eyes of a mother deer and her spotted fawn. They're just standing there watching us watching them, and I never would have guessed that Sammy Mack could ever be so quiet. It's like we all four have been caught in a photograph, like someone's sent a message. And it would go on like this all night except for the car in the road, hanging the curve. The headlights throw the deer from their pose. They escape on their skinny legs.

"Rudolph," Sammy says, when they're gone and

we're crossing the road.

"You think so?"

"Yup, I know so." He nods so vigorously that I worry he's going to snap a muscle, and now that we've reached his own driveway, he lets my battered finger go and heads off at a sprint for some old birches. "You wanna see what I can do?" he calls to me. I don't have so much as a chance to answer before he hurls himself up into the wishbone part of a tree and scrambles up its thickest branches.

"Impressive," I tell him, jogging now to where he is. "But more impressive for superheroes is the way they get back down."

"Easy," he tells me, and before I can stop him, he stands up tall on the branch he was sitting on and puts his arms out like wings. "To infinity and beyond!" he yells, and steps out into the night and falls through the air to the ground. He rolls around, a sidewise somersault. I rush toward him, swoop in.

"Flying is my specialty," Sammy says, all out of breath.

"Is that a fact?" He looks okay. He talks okay. He's standing up. He's walking. He takes off for his front door, and the door slams hard behind him, and suddenly I remember Sammy when he wasn't more than a single armful, when all he could do was lie in his carriage and wait to be lifted up toward the world. Mom and I would see them in town—Mrs. Mack and her bald baby boy. We'd be standing in line for a free chunk of fresh-baked bread at Basket or a whole sea bass at Hook and Sinker when we'd hear the boy fussing behind us, and wherever we were, whatever we had to do, however many bags we had in hand, Mom would walk straight back to where the Macks stood and offer to hold Sammy for a while.

"Can't keep him happy," Mrs. Mack would sigh as Mom unbuckled the stroller straps and lifted Sammy to her shoulder.

"Sometimes they just need a change of view," Mom would tell her.

There'd be gray shadows in the papery skin beneath Mrs. Mack's hard blue eyes, lengths of hair gone loose from a clip. "He hardly sleeps," Mrs. Mack would go on. "I wonder—sometimes I think—that I'm doing something wrong."

"This boy's just got a lot of living to do," Mom would assure her. "He's not planning on wasting a second," and as if to prove that Mom was right, Sammy would quiet down and look around, start pointing, gurgle noises.

"I guess," Mrs. Mack would say, and then, always, I don't know why: "Was Katie ever like that?"

"Katie was her own person," Mom would say, shifting Sammy in her arms, giving him more to point toward. "All of them are." And you know how you know a person's highest compliment? Well, this was Mom's. She wanted me always to be just who I am.

She wanted me never to pretend.

I stand a little longer under the cover of dark in Sammy's front yard, to be sure that the door doesn't fly open again. The kid seems safe for the night, safe for tonight, at least. I turn for home—myself, alone.

Chapter Fifteen

Two more days of rain, and on the third, Dad gets himself into a breakfast frenzy. On burner one, the pancakes; on burner two, the fried eggs; in all four slots of the toaster, toast; and on the table a bright purple dahlia. "What are you doing?" I ask him, and he says, "I was feeling inspired."

"Inspired?" I say. "Maybe more like hungry? You planning on chowing down all that yourself?"

"I was counting on your companionship," he says.

"My pancakes have never been better."

"Dad," I groan, grabbing my lunch, sealing it into Ziplocs.

"Even brainiacs need sustenance," he says. "Probably even more than your average joe."

"Right," I say, and I pull out a chair. "But only one, okay?"

"Some OJ with that?"

"Sure, some OJ. Okay."

"And an egg? Just one? Just the littlest one?"

"All right, Dad. Okay. Just one egg."

"You wouldn't be in the mood for toast, by any chance?"

"No, Dad. No toast. Not today."

"Now," he says, choosing a tumbler from the cupboard, and looking only a little sad about my saying no to toast, "tell me about Friday. You never did say much."

"Friday? You mean the library?" There's such a

pour-down of kitchen sun that I have trouble, for a sec, dialing the details back—the rain, the Local Lore, Danny's surprise hello. "Yeah, well," I say, after Dad puts the filled-to-the-brim tumbler down at my place, "Friday was interesting. Friday was newspapers. All the circa stuff." I decide not to mention Danny, because if I mention Danny, Dad will start back in on Jessie and Ellen—asking me, for the millionth time, when Jessie is coming over to talk her blue streak, when Ellen is going to arrive and trip up the stairs and say "Sorry," as if the stairs need apologizing to, when we all are going out together, when we are coming back from the mall together, stupid things in our glossy bags, like boas or triple-sized sunglasses.

"Any leads?"

"She had the lead in a Shakespeare play at Baldwin," I say, and Dad says, "Ha-ha."

"No," I continue. "Seriously. Plus, she was Miss Independence Day in the Fourth of July parade. In 1946 there was a sledding party at her house. Her mother's victory garden won a prize in 1942. Best tomatoes. Best asparagus. Lima beans the size of a baby's fingernail."

"Nothing much, in other words," Dad says. He's sat down now, has sliced his butter onto his pancake, poured himself a lake of syrup, downed half of his OJ. He nods in the direction of my plate, the old get-started-you-disappoint-me-how-little-you-eat nod. I know it well.

"Nothing too useful, anyway." I break a first bite of pancake with the side of my fork. It's not gooey like the last time he threw batter into a pan. He's definitely improving.

"I see. Any manifestations of John Butler Ever-last?"

"Manifestations?"

"You know, in the newspapers. Did his name come up?"

"Some," I say, trying to remember the things that

Danny reported. "Mergers and growth at Quality Chemicals. Businessman of the Year from the Chamber of Commerce. Prize border collie. Library donor."

"Nothing about his paintings?"

"No. Nothing like that."

"Any sponsorship of any art galleries or wings of art museums?"

"Not yet, anyway."

"Any personal bests in local art shows?"

"Dad," I moan, "don't you think I'd have said so?"

"You're keeping an eye out, though?"

"Of course." I nod self-assuredly, so that he doesn't ask again.

"You like the pancake?" he asks.

"Perfect, Dad."

"You mean that?"

"Absolutely."

"You know," he says, "this farmer's-market syrup. It makes all the difference."

I look at the watch on my wrist and the clock behind Dad, which never come close to agreement. I stand, collect my dishes. "Gonna be late, Dad."

"All right."

Leaning back in his chair, he makes a sad little face at my half-eaten pancake and the yolk that I have left on my plate. There is still a pile of pancakes on his plate, and I get that guilty feeling right in my gut for leaving him alone to eat like this, nothing to talk to except the dahlia. I stop and lean down, give his forehead a kiss. "How about you, Dad?" I ask him. "Making headway?"

"Funny thing about that painting," he says.

"What's that?"

"The varnish," he says. "Subtle, but it's there: a pattern of *Iris pseudacorus*."

"You mean like fleurs-de-lis?" I say.

"The very same."

"Well that's odd," I say.

"Yes, I thought so, too. To pattern a painting with flowers, like he did, but to eliminate their color. To make them varnish only. It made me wonder."

"Dad?" I say as my pulse quickens.

"What is it?"

"The thing is—in the write up of Miss Martine's debutante ball? The reporter said that she was carrying fleurs-de-lis."

"Is that right?"

"And didn't Mom use to tell a story about King Clovis and his army and a river and these flowers that stood out in the river like a guide? Those flowers that saved him being the very same fleurs-de-lis."

"That was one version of that story," Dad says, nodding slowly, rubbing the skin beneath one eye. "Very interesting, Katie. Increasingly so."

"Maybe, but I still don't know what it means."

"Well, that Miss Martine loved yellow irises, for one thing."

"Maybe still does."

"Ever see them over at the estate?"

"Not really," I say. "Not that I remember."

"Take a good look around," he tells me. "Report back. Flower heads would be gone by now, but there should be evidence of stalks."

"I will," I say. "Absolutely."

"You're a fine investigator, Miss Katie," he tells me now. "Don't know what I'd do without you."

"Bet this is going to be a breakthrough day," I say.

"For you or for me?" His face lightens.

"For the D'Amores," I say. "The both of us."

"Maybe so," he says.

"I'll get the dishes later if you just leave them in the sink." I grab my stuff and head out the door, find my bike, adjust my backpack, set off down the drive. I'm halfway there when I see Sammy Mack down by the mailbox, kicking up some gravel.

"Hey," I call to him, skidding my bike to a stop.

"Sammy! What's up?"

"Nothing," he says.

"Nothing? Did you cross the street all by your-self?"

He nods one big I'm-a-hero nod, like yes is the right answer to this question. He has yesterday's jeans on and an even worse T-shirt, and the laces of his hero shoes are flipped out in all directions. I am thinking that his mother doesn't even know that he's gone. I'm thinking she's over there dreaming.

"That's dangerous, Sammy. You shouldn't."

"Jimmy needs me," he says, and it takes me a min-ute to realize that he's talking about my dad.

"Jimmy does?"

"Yup." He pumps his chin up and down again.

"Well, that's fine, Sammy, if that's what you think. But you shouldn't cross the road alone, okay? And you should always tell your mother where you're going." I start to climb down from my bike to tighten his sloppy laces, but he takes off like a demon down the drive, toward the house and studio.

"You can't make me go home," he yells out. "You can't, you can't, you can't."

"Sammy!" I call to him. "Sammy, come here. Let's fix your laces." But by now Dad has heard the commotion, and he's stepped into the drive.

"Well, if it isn't Mr. Mack," I hear him say.

"First-rate assistant," Sammy says.

"You like pancakes?"

"You got syrup?"

"Yes, my man. I just happen to be rich in syrup."

"I like you, Jimmy."

"And I like you back, Mr. Mack."

Chapter Sixteen

F lying down the hill past the twisty trees and the stone posts and the black gates and the gardens, scanning for the bottom parts of irises because now I just can't help myself, I suddenly remember the day before Barcelona, when Jessie and Ellen showed up early and told my mother that they'd come to kidnap me. Mom was out in the garden with her nightgown on, which was more like a slip, which made me think, whenever she wore it, that if she hadn't grown up with so many horses, she'd have grown up a ballerina. Her arms were long and really thin and pale, and her bracelets were always flinging off and bouncing straight across the floor—too loose for her super-tiny wrists. The diamond she wore on her left hand slid around and around beneath her knuckle, so that most of the time it looked like she wore a simple golden band. She went barefooted in the house and in the garden, too, and she always watered before the sun was too high, holding the hose close to the roots of things, plucking out weeds, picking out a table bud, and never, ever worrying about her hair, which was always lopsided when she climbed out of bed. My mom loved yellow flowers, too. She liked the surprise, each year, that burst from bulbs.

When Jessie and Ellen biked up, she said, "Girls," and hugged them both, like they were her other two daughters, which you could kind of say they were, because they'd been my friends since kindergarten, since bus rides and since Brownies, since the camping trip where it rained for three days and we all——my dad, my mom, my friends——sat in a tent telling each other stupid stories. "Girls." I was downstairs in the kitchen, and I saw them out there, my two best friends with their wind-mussed hair and my mom with her nightgown and garden hose. They talked a lot before my mom showed them in, and then we all sat around having breakfast, and this was all forever and ever ago, when my dad still slept upstairs and had his pancakes waiting for him, his toast in the toaster, his Claire in her own chair, and he'd come down late, with his floppy hair, and say, "Morning," putting on a pair of glasses to see what he could see.

After that, Jessie, Ellen, and I biked up the hills and soared down the hills into town, single file. Town around here is just an intersection with shops stretching over and then the other way, but mostly it's this one corner with two benches where everybody goes, and somebody always has a guitar or a harmonica or something, and we all stand around drinking coffee from the Gryphon, the local coffee shop. There's a movie theater right there, three doors down, which was once, I think, an opera house or something, decorated and fancy, and in the morning, in the summers, they open up for Kids' Club, playing old kid-rated movies for free.

The day before Barcelona, the three of us went to the movies at ten o'clock—stood in line with all the little kids and their moms and their nannies, because it was ridiculous and we knew it, because it was cool inside and hot everywhere else, because we could sit in the back with our shoes kicked off and a bucket of popcorn and a box of Skittles between us. The thing is, I can't remember the movie we watched, I can only remember us laughing, Jessie laughing so hard that she almost fell to the floor from her chair and Ellen saying, "Oh my God Oh my God Oh my God," like she was trapped inside a giant hiccup.

I was the luckiest person in the whole wide world, and I didn't know it, and here's what I hate about being so smart: My smartness counts for nothing. I didn't know, I couldn't guess, that that was to be the last easy fun I'd ever have with the two best friends I'll ever know. Two days after we got home from Barcelona, my father took my mother to the doctor— piled her into the car because she couldn't fight him anymore, because she couldn't keep her secret any longer. Four weeks after that, the doctors were sure. Everything looks like caution afterward, everything inside me feels old and used and cracked, and people say, "Oh, Katie, you've handled your mother's passing so well," and I think, *Handled. Handled? I'm barely breathing, can't you tell?* And somewhere out there Jessie and Ellen are laughing, just the two of them, in the back of an old theater, and they think that I've forgotten them, maybe, but I haven't. I never would—they just remind me of my mother, they just ask about my mother, and that's not a question I want to hear, even if I knew how to answer.

My mom would know how to break the painting code.

My mom would know where the yellow flags grow, and why a woman who could have had anything would carry them into her debutante ball.

Chapter *Seventeen*

The weekend's rain steams up from the ground, like dragon's breath. I veer inside the entrance gates at Miss Martine's, swoop across the macadam, hop off the bike, and start walking, taking longer breaths now to slow my heart down. I pass Amy on my way to the machine shed, and she waves her hat at me. Yvonne's a little way off, with buckets in her hands that look full of squirming green snakes, but actually, I see it now, they're only full of ferns. "Girl!" she yells up at me, since she can't wave, and I say, "Good morning, Miss Yvonne. What did you think of all that rain?"

"Got my laundry done, anyway," she calls back. "But, man, did we get rain-socked." She nods her head in the down-the-slope direction, and I look with her. From here the grass looks like a little bit of green in a lot of water crystals, and the heads of the flowers and trees are bowing low. The stream is a crooked line of blue-brown that looks wider than usual, spilled out over its sides. Near the hole I make out Old Olson, Ida, Reny, the Santopolos—all of them in a circle, looking down at something.

"What's going on over there?" I ask Yvonne.

"You've got me." She shrugs. "I'm on dividing duty."

I roll my bike into the shed, flick down the kick-stand, and cut across the hill, under the sun, soaking the toes of my work boots, hearing the water sloshing into my socks, looking around for the aftermath of irises, if there are irises at the garden at all. The crossing stones are pretty much sunk below the stream. I have to walk back to where the bridge is, cross there, walk down to the others. The hole looks like the espresso my father makes himself in the morning—caramel-colored. Still, all this time, the team's been standing there staring, and finally I can hear the conversation.

"Definitely culminating project material," Owen's saying. "I mean, it's gotta be prehistoric."

"Who teaches science anyway, these days?" asks Ida. "Prehistoric? Are you kidding?"

"When's the last time you've seen a turtle shell this perfect?" Owen asks back.

"Prehistoric does not mean one year pre me," says Ida, and Reny laughs, a good-for-Ida laugh. She gives him a look that's a combo of I've known you forever and Okay, I admit, you're half decent.

"Hey, Katie," Danny says when he hears me sloshing forward. "Check this out." He steps aside, making room for me in the circle. Owen shoves his turtle shell at me. Half a turtle shell, I guess it is. The carapace.

"Cool," I say. It feels so good standing right here next to Danny that I could pretty much end up talking turtles all day. "Where did you find it?" I reach for the shell, and Owen lets me hold it in my hands. I turn it over and over—bowl to hill and back to bowl—and only when I turn it a third time do I feel what seems like a prick point in the underside. I trace the indentation with my index finger. I flip the carapace over and read the mark by the light of the sun. Odd, I think. The things you discover in a garden.

"Noticed part of it sticking up over there," he's saying, making an exaggerated gesture toward one corner of the hole. "Didn't know what it was, so started digging." The mud is still wet on his arms and his knees. He's got a streak across his face where he must have smacked a bug. "Pulled it up and nothing's broken. Nothing. It's perfect."

"He's building his own museum," Reny says, who's been slapping at bugs the whole time Owen's been talking, and annoying the heck out of Ida.

"And he's charging us admission," Ida says now.

"You're just jealous," Owen says, "because you didn't find it."

Danny leans toward me and stays that way. He turns his head, whispers through his curls. "Something else has shown up," he tells me. "But I'll catch you later." He puts his finger to his lips and smiles. I feel a shiver going up and down all the little bone chunks of my spine, and I can't tell, even within myself, if the shiver is for Danny, for this something else he's found, or for the mark scratched into the carapace. I look at the sludge of a hole, not pretty, and then at Old Olson, who hasn't said a single thing all this time about the turtle shell, nor the mud, nor the buckets he's got piled up on the back of his cart, which I'm guessing he won't have to explain; buckets are for scooping rain out of a disgusting hole of mud. What is he thinking? Why does he hang here, like he does, wanting us to dig but nervous with us digging, all stone-cold silent about Owen's carapace? His eyes are hard as metal; that's what it is. The blue and the black of them are confused as a bruise.

They're the color, too, of the old slate tiles that make the roof on the caretaker's house where Old Olson lives, just down the drive from Miss Martine's, hidden behind a garden. You'd have to walk under a trellis to get to his front door. Crawl over the window boxes to get inside his windows. His whole little house is so garden protected that the most open-door it gets is by way of its roof, which is so steep and so pitched that even Sammy Mack would, I'm guessing, think twice before accepting an invitation to stomp all over it.

Reny's the one who finally says, "Well, the shell sure is a fascination, but shall we get to work?"

Danny tilts in the opposite direction. "Sure," he says.

I tip back and catch my balance.

"Where're we floating the old floodwaters?" Ida asks, heading off to the cart to collect herself a bucket.

"Skim the top, take it down to the stream," Old Olson says.

"Don't touch my shell," Owen tells Danny, as he cradles it in between the branches of a tree.

"Wouldn't think of it, bro," Danny tells him. Seriously. Sometimes you can't even believe that the two of them are just one year apart.

We're so mud mired by the time lunch comes around that we all head off for a wash and then for a break; Old Olson says that we've worked so hard he's going to give us an extra hour. I'm thinking that he wants that hour to himself, to do his own exploring.

At Miss Martine's, the hired help has its own lavatory system—a lineup of bathrooms plopped down at the back of the greenhouse that sits right against the property's edge. You have to go through the greenhouse to get to the bathrooms, and this time of year the air inside the greenhouse is like the place inside a laundry iron where the water you pour in turns to steam. It's mostly empty buckets and a couple of lemon trees, lots of starter vegetables, and a row of baby seedlings. When we hit the greenhouse, we aren't talking. We push through the door, single file, into the concrete hall where four doors lead to four toilets and sinks. It's a unisex operation. You wait in line. I got here last, so I'm waiting. I listen to four spigots going off at once, and now Reny starts singing another one of his tunes, whistling the melody between the words he can remember. I don't even want to think about what the sinks are going to look like when I get my turn. It's only dirt, I tell myself, and water.

Finally Ida comes out looking scrubbed as a pot, the rim of her T-shirt a fresh wet collar. Ida has skin that could be earth all cracked to pieces by summer. The lines don't resemble anything close to a direction; they just break out every which way, some on the surface, some much deeper. I can't imagine Ida young, can't believe she was ever my age, ever doing anything womanlike to get Reny to come over and notice. She's just a block of who she is, no decoration, and she stares at me like I'm the odd one.

"Girl," she says, "you could use a scrubbing."

"Yeah," I say. "No doubt."

"Sink's all yours. Left you a little dab of Ivory."

"Thanks," I say, but *Gross*, I think. Soap after Ida. Disgusting.

In the bathroom, I turn the water full blast to wash away the crust of Ida's cleanup. My face is huge in the narrow mirror, all mud zapped and dried out, and I start scrubbing. My hands first, then my arms to my elbows, then my elbows to my T-shirt sleeve, then my kneecaps, then up to my face, going real easy on the Ivory, because there's hardly even a dab; Ida must have really gone all at it. I shake my hair out of Danny's cap, try to fix it with my fingers, but my hair has a mind of its own—you wouldn't call it curly, which would be nice, or even wavy. It just doesn't do what I want it to do, so I roll it back up into Danny's cap and pull the bill down, snug. I dial the faucet knobs back to off, pull open the door, and there is Danny, waiting.

"Hey," I say, feeling the warm crawl of a blush across my face, wishing I had the mud back on, to hide it.

"Hey." He opens the door to the greenhouse, stands back, says, "Ladies first." I walk the skinny aisle with Danny right behind me. I walk and he's so close, and the greenhouse air's so hot, so tight.

"So Owen's got a turtle shell," I say, to break the silence.

"Culminating project," Danny says. "What was yours?"

"I don't know," I say, and I'm about to tell Danny something more about my research, all my questions, but he takes the conversation somewhere else.

"What do you mean, you don't know?"

"Well, I mean, I *know,* but it was kind of strange."

"So? Tell me."

"God," I sigh, and we're through the greenhouse now, we're getting to the door, we're out in the real air, under the sky. Danny steps beside me, and I feel the ache of the morning dig lift away and vanish.

"Come on," he says.

"Barcelona," I tell him. "I wrote about it. First-person travelogue."

"What's so strange about that?"

"It wasn't the Barcelona that everybody sees. My Barcelona was underground, the place where the city begins." I wait for him to laugh, but he doesn't. We just

∗∗ 144 ∗∗

keep walking, the rest of everybody all gone off who knows where, the trees beside the stream throwing down their shade, and Danny waiting. "My mom and my dad and me," I start, but I don't even know where to start. "Last summer," I say, and he says, "Yeah. I heard. You went away."

"Yeah," I say. "We did." And I know that people talked back then. I know that people talked through the fall and through the whole month of December, when I didn't go a single day to school, when I stayed home and sat with my mom in her room with the colors. I just didn't know that Danny had been listening. I mean, I hardly knew him.

"So where does Barcelona begin?" he asks. "Your Barcelona? The one you wrote about?"

I say, "Do you want to sit down for a while?" I start walking toward the stream, and Danny follows. We each find a stone to settle upon. Mine is mostly moss, some granite. Danny's stone has its back flat against a tree.

"You want to hear the weird thing about Barcelona?" I ask him.

"What's that?"

"It keeps its ghosts underground."

Danny laughs. "You know for a fact?"

"I do," I say. "I saw them."

Now Danny pushes back against the tree, fits his arms across his chest, and waits for me to explain about the ghosts, which is one of the things that I appreciate about Danny. He's not the kind who's always looking for ways to push himself into the talk, not all Look at me, not My story's better than yours. He has patience, and I like that about him, and maybe it would be okay right now, because it's just the two of us, and because he asked, to tell him something about the day my mom and I climbed down beneath the streets of Barcelona, to find the other Barcelona, the one the Romans built two thousand years ago, and the Iberians before that. The one I wrote about.

That Barcelona is under glass, inside the thickest walls I've ever seen, and cool when up above it's broiling hot. Everything down there in the ghost world is lit orange and yellow with big glow lights that make it seem like day is fighting with night. Fine lines. They have fourth-century-B.C. goddess heads down there. Iron swords. Sewing needles made out of bone. Beds and candles, oil lamps, hinges and locks and keys, and places in the walls where little god statues stood, beckoning to the souls of the dead. What my mother loved, what she couldn't stop staring at, were the rooms they called the cubicula, tiny private rooms with a bed and a chest and a chair, and the most beautiful, most delicate containers for makeup. There were mortars for mashing colors and spatulas for mixing and carved combs and flasks made out of glass. "Can't you see them?" my mother said, and I said, "Who?"

"These women," she answered.

"The Romans?"

She nodded. "Yes." Her eyes were so wide and her face was so pale and right then she was just as much a ghost as they were. If my mother could have walked through glass, she'd have walked straight through to the other side, to one of those little rooms, and sat right down on one of those little chairs and I would have seen, I swear to God, the Roman women talking to my mother, beauty to beauty, infinitely beautiful, forever. She stood staring at the cubicula for such a long, long time. After that she found a bench.

"You okay?" I asked her, and that's the thing: She didn't answer, and she was honest, and why didn't I notice, why did I say, right after that: "Dad's probably packing; we should go"?

"Honey," she said, "remember this. Remember how alive we are now." I do remember, and that's what I mean: In Barcelona there are ghosts.

"Well, that was a good story," Danny says, and I realize that I've been sitting here saying nothing. I feel my whole face turn red, and my neck, also my arms.

"God," I say. "I'm sorry." I look straight into his wide eyes and wish that I had a way of explaining, that I hadn't just been sitting here on a rock, halfway to Barcelona. He looks back into me. Smiles, lifts his shoulders, and shrugs.

"Someday," I say, "I'll tell you about Barcelona. I just can't right now."

"I'm cool with chilling." Danny lifts his arm and it falls across my shoulders. He pulls me close and I fold—my bones, my skin, everything I am, pressed up against him.

"You want to hear the other news of the day?" he finally asks.

"Yeah." I nod. "I do."

"Headline version," Danny says. "Miss Martine didn't show up at her father's funeral."

"Wait," I say. "How do you know that?"

Danny takes his arm from across my shoulders and

digs into his big back pocket, a huge, cavernous space, from what I can tell, where you could pack a picnic and then some. After a lot of shoveling around, he pulls out a square of newsprint.

"You stole from Local Lore?" I ask, appalled and a little thrilled and maybe confused at the same time as he spreads the paper on the ground at our feet. I can't understand where the thing has come from. I was sitting right there beside Danny the whole time at the library, except for the end, when I went to ask Ms. McDermott a question.

"Only borrowing," Danny says. "I plan to give it back."

"Well, why didn't you *say* something? Before, I mean."

"As I recall, you were doing all the talking."

He leans down, and I do, too, squinting to read the paper in the sun. It's one huge feature on John Butler Everlast. His obituary, plus the gossip, plus a list of every person who came to show respects.

"Jesus, Danny."

"Says that he died in 1973, cause of death pneumonia," Danny continues. "Says his memorial service was one for the books. Says a thousand people came, but do you see Miss Martine's name anywhere in that list? You see her in any of the pictures?"

I scan the whole page. I stop and read it slow. Danny is right.

"Where was she, then?" he asks me. "How do you explain it?"

"I don't know." I shake my head, plant my elbows on my knees, hold up my head with my fists. "They had a fight? She was pissed off? She was out of the country? She was sick?" Danny starts folding the newsprint back into its crackling squares. He leans forward, touches my cheek.

"We have another clue," he says, smiling his extremely white smile.

"Another ticket to nowhere."

"We just need more clues. Power in numbers."

When he stands, I stand beside him. When he walks, I walk, too, and now I'm thinking how nice it is not to walk alone, not to stand apart, not to face the big questions on my own.

"You ever hear the story about King Clovis?" I ask as we veer closer to the stream.

"Honors history, Mr. Larson. Guy stranded at a river. Flowers show him the way. Fleurs-de-lis, right? Rescue and escape? Why do you ask?"

"It's just that Miss Martine carried fleurs-de-lis at her debutante ball, and fleurs-de-lis are yellow flag irises, and yellow flag irises grow in swamps." I leave the Everlast painting out of this for now; we're nearly back at the site, and there wouldn't be time to explain. "Why would the daughter of one of the richest men on the whole Main Line carry irises, if she could have orchids, or roses? What did the fleurs-de-lis mean?"

"That she liked yellow irises?"

"I don't know. Maybe. Or maybe that she was looking for an out."

"Out of what?"

"Out of this." I sweep my hands toward the garden estate, and Danny shakes his head.

"Who'd want out of this?" he asks. "Look around," he says. "Look up. It's really kind of perfect."

"You're a funny guy," I say.

"Why's that?"

"Because most guys wouldn't have noticed."

"Katie, listen. The woman lives in a house on a hill alone, and she's lived there all her life. That doesn't sound like escape to me. That sounds like a choice."

"I guess," I say, though I'm not convinced, but now there's no more time to debate it. We've made our way back to where it all begins—to the mud, and our shovels and axes.

Chapter *Eighteen*

All afternoon, digging and sweating, I'm thinking about Danny. About Danny, about the clues, about Barcelona, about a daughter who doesn't show up at a father's funeral. About varnish and color and disappeared color. About rescue and escape and Miss Martine, who maybe, if she strained hard enough, could see the dig from where she is, inside her house. Her dig. The sun pushes itself between the trees, insists on its own heat, and it feels like we're working inside a pot of stew. There's dirt and sticks and bug shells at my feet, and beneath Danny's cap my hair is ruinous. By the time the shift is done, we're all too tired to do much more than head for home.

In the kitchen there's the in-the-oven-smell of pot roast, but everything is strangely quiet. I finally find my father on the living-room couch, no TV on. He seems asleep, but his eyes are open—staring at the ceiling, no glasses on. I used to find him like this every day for weeks after my mother died, until finally he began to work again, began to cook, like someone far away and maybe high above us was forcing him back to life.

"You okay?" I ask him.

He says quietly, "Hey, Katie."

I tromp over to the couch, sit at one end, near his toes, untie my heavy, old, grunge-ugly work boots, which I will, I promise myself, dump in the trash once this garden gig is over. "What's happening, Dad?"

"It's that painting," he says.

I wait for him to tell me more, to roll his eyeballs back down from the ceiling. It's way too hot in the house, thanks to that pot roast. I feel drips of sweat running down my neck, down my tee. I get up to shove open a window. "If you wanted to paint regret," Dad asks at last, "what symbol would you use?"

"Regret?" I'm too confused, tired, hot to fake an answer.

"Things that you wished you could do over. How would you paint that?"

"I don't know."

"It's a theoretical question, Katie. It's not like I'm going to hold you to the answer."

"Regret could be a bird flying away," I say, thinking out loud, playing this game for his sake, because for all I know he's been lying here for hours, waiting to ask. "Or it could be the shell you leave on the beach, or maybe the last leaf on a tree."

"Would you paint a perfect city and give the whole thing a brown-black sky?" Dad asks.

"Is this a trick question?"

"Would you paint all the windows in the city black, except for one light in a single room?"

"I thought you said this painting was Everlast's idea of the eternal."

"I thought the darkness was dirt, but it's not."

"So this city of Everlast's is dark?"

"Dark, except for the garden."

"There's a garden?"

"Pink, yellow, green, orange, ochre, violet, Tuscan red."

"You can see that much already, Dad? You've already done that much work?"

"I'm starting to see *through*," he corrects me. "There's a difference."

"Well, is the garden *the* garden? The one at Miss Martine's?"

"I'm thinking it might be."

"Does it have a stream?

"Yes, a finger of a stream."

"Is Miss Martine herself in the painting?"

"No, or at least I can't see her yet."

I take all this in. I try to fit the parts together. I understand, a little more, why Dad's been lying here staring.

"Dad," I ask now, keeping my voice still and cool as I can make it, "is there, like, a turtle in the painting?"

"A turtle?"

"A turtle. You know, with a shell?"

"There are many things I still can't quite make out," he says after a spell of not moving, not breathing, just lying there thinking, like he does. "One of those things could be a turtle. Why do you ask?"

"At the garden today—at the dig? Owen found a carapace. It was cool and everything, you know—just the shell itself was cool—but then when I was holding it, I found the thing had this mark in the back. An indentation. Had to be put there."

He smiles.

"I'm serious, Dad."

He sits there rubbing his chin, working out something, but I am not even going to guess what. There's never a point to rushing genius.

"Dad," I ask after some time goes by. "What kind of daughter doesn't go to her own father's funeral?"

Abruptly he turns toward me, and the reverie is gone. He gives me a scary, intense stare. "That's an odd question," he says. "Why do you ask?"

"Because that's what happened with Miss Martine. Everlast died, the town came to pay respects, but not Miss Martine. It's in the record, at the library," I add. I leave out the part about Danny.

"Strange," Dad says, and now his face changes again, his eyes go unfocused, and I realize that he still hasn't chosen a pair of glasses to put on. A thousand thoughts go through his mind—I can see the flutter. He sits there blinking at them and doesn't tell me one.

"Do you know when the painting was finished?" I ask.

"From what I can make out so far, 1960."

"Miss Martine hasn't been seen since 1954."

"You have the month and day?"

"Reny said something about September 10, the day of a massive storm."

"Well there's your answer, Katie D'Amore. Recluses don't go out, even to the funerals of their fathers." He plants his feet on the floor, fishes up some eyeglasses from the chains around his neck, puts on a pair, gives me a long, funny look, then winks. "Nineteen fifty-four," he repeats now, then says nothing else.

"Yeah. Right."

"You should be learning everything you can about that one particular day, Katie. Seems like there's something in it."

"Could be," I say, though of course he's right.

"I think I'm killing the pot roast," he says, pushing himself off the couch. "Better go and take a look."

"Hey," I say.

"What?"

"Thanks."

I can tell that he wants to move on to something new, that whatever he was feeling when I first came home is still floating here, above us. "Where's Sammy?" I change the subject.

"His mother came and got him, some time around four."

"Is he still your first-rate assistant?" I follow Dad to the kitchen, which is smoking by now. It feels like he's far away, and what I want, right now, is to reel him back. "Did he like your breakfast?"

"Ate three and a half pancakes."

"That all?"

"Almost ran me out of syrup."

"He's crazy, you know."

"He's just a kid, Katie."

"You're like his second father, Dad."

Dad gives me another one of his looks, gets a little red around the ears. "Nothing of the sort," he says. "Just an old mad scientist with a funky day job." He pulls the tumblers out of the cabinet. I go and get the lemonade. I set the table for the two of us. There's just one rose in the vase tonight.

Later the steam that has been rising all day long has made a sticky clump in the green bowl of my room. Nothing sweet blows through the window. No breeze bumps up the stairs. "Nineteen fifty-four," I repeat, whirling the year around in my head. I think of all the research to do, the codes to break, the hours between now and tomorrow, between knowing and not knowing, between me and me seeing Danny.

I try to cool myself down by thinking of Niagara Falls and the Pacific Ocean, of buckets of ice and frosted soda, of the day Jessie and Ellen and I climbed over the fence of the Henrys' house down the street and swam late at night in their pool; they never noticed, they were gone, living for the summer in their Aruba getaway. Jessie did a mean Henrys imitation. Ellen climbed back over the fence the very next day and left them a pot of thank-you flowers.

I never liked the Henrys, but that night I loved their pool, and now I'm thinking of that park with the pools in Barcelona, which was past the Gothic quarter, up near the arch and the bocce pits, where some guy with a hat took my dad aside and said something about the thievery of the Moors. "That can't be right," my mother said, but Dad stood by his translation, Dad said he knew what he'd been told but that didn't mean that he believed it, and then we were still walking, or maybe we had turned and were headed back, but suddenly there we were in this park of a million water fountains and a million kids running and splashing in their underwear. There was this bald guy wearing bright feathers for hair. There was this other guy with a pink scarf who was making music with a horn so long that it hit the ground and turned up and kept rising.

Deeper in on the path that wound up and down by all those millions of pools was a gazebo, maybe the size of Miss Martine's, but higher off the ground, and right there was dancing. It was like the dancers used their feet to dust the floor, like their only words were the words of the song that played from the boom box some kid had brought along. I watched them for a long time.

I was watching the dancers when my parents drifted away. I turned and didn't see them and walked under some trees, and up a pile of steps, and through this sculpture where dragons carved of stone sat spraying water high, and then I went down the stones, and under some flowered trees and over past some cats. I finally found them down where a wedding was going on, or had already happened, my mother sitting on a bench, my dad beside her, both of them watching this bride and her groom at the edge of a pond where the water was so still I could have sworn it was a mirror. I saw my mom pull a flower straight out of a tree. I saw her stand, take the flower to the bride, and bow her head. I saw her go back to the bench and sit down with my dad and ask him, "Would you marry me again, Jimmy? Would you?"

"In a heartbeat," he said, "and you know it."

"I wouldn't take any of it back," Mom said, and maybe I don't know how you put regret inside a painting, maybe I can't figure out Miss Martine, maybe I can't really save my dad from sadness, but maybe so much time goes by that you start to understand how beauty and sadness can both live in one place. My eyes are heavy and the air is still hot. I may already be dreaming.

Chapter

S ammy sits on top of two fat phone books, and
now he points his fork straight down like a pole
and jiggles the French toast around until a piece
breaks off. He swishes it through a pool of syrup.

"You're way early, aren't you, Sammy?" I ask, looking at Dad.

"My dad brought me."

"Your *dad* brought you?"

"Yeah. He was going to the airport." Sammy's got

a Phillies shirt on and a pair of red shorts. His light-up sneaks are kicking at the air above the floor.

"How's my daughter detective?" Finally Dad says something, holding a plate toward me that has just one piece of French toast. "There's plenty more," he says, "if you want it."

"This is enough." I sigh, taking my place between Sammy and Dad, pushing my hair back from my face.

"Sammy's been telling me stories," Dad says.

"Uh-huh." The French toast is good.

"Super bullet yellow bird," Sammy says. He points his fork upright and starts spinning it around, throwing globs of buttery syrup everywhere.

"What did you say?" I ask.

"*Brrrrrrrrrr,*" Sammy says, loud as a drill. "*Brrrrrrrrrrrr.*" He's stabbing his fork at every last open spot of air, his lower lip jutting out and vibrating. I stare at him, wondering what he's seen, if the finch hammers at his window, too.

"I think Katie gets the idea," Dad says, touching Sammy's hand with his own to chill the demonstration.

"Where's the bird, Sammy?" I ask him.

"Outside." He jabs his fork toward the window.

"Where outside?"

"*Outside* outside." He points again, then sticks the fork into his mouth and chews with his mouth wide open. His teeth are the tiniest teeth I've ever seen, but fierce.

"Can you show me?"

"Katie," Dad says, "I just got him settled in. And you've hardly touched your French toast."

"Well, after you're done eating, Sammy. Can you?" I give Dad the I-know-what-I'm-doing look. Now he's the exasperated one.

"I can show you right now!" Sammy shouts, throwing his fork to his plate, jumping off his phone-book tower, and heading for the door. Dad puts his head into his hands.

"Sorry, Dad," I say. "We'll be right back, I promise." I push back my chair and hurry to catch up with Sammy, who has already slammed the door behind him. Out in the middle of the driveway he's stomping, around and around, waiting for me to stand beside him.

"Right there," he says now, pointing high, not in the direction of his house, but in the direction of mine, in the direction, to be specific, of my parents' bedroom window. I follow his hand and that's precisely where he's pointing, no question about it. He stomps around some more now, mission accomplished. I put both of my hands on his little mighty shoulders until he finally looks up at me.

"Sammy," I say, "tell me exactly what you mean."

"Super bullet yellow bird," Sammy says. "Going *brrrrrrrrrrrr brrrrrrrrrrrrrrr brrrrrrrrrrrrrrrrrrrrrrr* at the window."

"That window?" I point to my parents' room.

"Yup."

"When?"

"When I came with Dad."

"You mean this morning, Sammy? Early?"

"Today!" he shouts. "Today! Today!" There's no way on earth that this kid is lying, and suddenly I understand. The window finch is a messenger. There is something that it wants to say.

"Man, you really are a first-rate assistant," I tell Sammy, and he smiles ear to ear, showing off all those baby teeth, shaking his shoulders so that my hands come loose.

"I have superhero powers," he says.

"I guess you do."

He nods ferociously. "I do."

"We better go inside and finish breakfast," I say. "My dad's going to need you fortified."

"Fortified?" Sammy asks, his nose wrinkled. He turns and marches backward across the drive, into the house.

"Superhero plus," I say.

Chapter Twenty

Now that it's the sweet time of day and the sun feels good on my skin, I don't mind just sitting here on these library steps watching the traffic go by, don't mind the fact that I'll be late to Miss Martine's and the dig, that I'll likely catch Old Olson's flack. I don't mind watching the clouds break and drift, and sometimes it looks like there are signals up high, and sometimes the sky is through-and-through blue, and it's really pretty out here in the morning, by myself, alone. Beauty and sadness. Rescue and escape. There's that line, I think, between what is and what has not happened yet.

It's a little past eight thirty when I see a red Miata slow and take the library parking-lot turn. A few minutes more and I hear the *clack-clack*ing of Ms. McDermott's tall, flare-heeled sandals. Every single one of her toenails is painted a different shade of red, all in service to her skirt, which is like a big flamenco costume—sunset colors seamed with black, a magnificent volume that coils and uncoils about her legs. Her black tank top seems to skim her skin. She pulls her sunglasses to the top of her head, changing the angles of her hair, and when she moves her arm, her big bag falls down, into the crook of her elbow.

"Katie D'Amore," she says, shading her eyes with her hand. "Aren't we bright and early?" She makes a little music with the dangle of her keys, and for one shining moment she's framed by the sun.

"Sorry," I say.

"No need," she says. She continues up the steps, the bright wings of her skirt flapping behind her, and I stand to follow, wait for her to open the door. Now we're the only two in the entire library—us and a civilization's worth of books. A full bin of returned books sits under the slot at the door. She gives it a quick once-over, hits the lights, makes her way to the circulation desk.

"So what brings you to our fine institution at this early hour?" she wants to know. She walks ahead of me and I let her, embarrassed to be looked at from behind. I'm dressed for work, after all. Crud clothes.

"A date," I tell her.

"A date?" she asks. "Or a year?"

I blush. "The second."

She's moved around to her side of the desk and tossed her keys into her bag. Now she replaces her shades with her reading glasses and rebuckles the strap of one shoe. "Fashion," she says, "is killing." She stands up straight and tests the shoe. Her whole skirt dances away from her, returns. She belongs, I'm thinking, on Fifth Avenue. Anywhere but here, and most definitely not alone.

"I wouldn't know," I tell her, and though I don't mean much by the comment, she stops and gives me a long, steady look, head to toe. Me—grubbed-out me—in my work boots and khakis, my worn-out T-shirt, my Danny BU cap, which hides my hair.

"You could know, Katie, if you wanted to. You could wear anything well."

I look at myself, rub at a spot on my shirt, push a stray strand of hair from my face. "You're an unusual librarian," I finally tell her.

"Yes," she says, smiling. "I've heard that before."

"I mean, you're all dressed up, and your audience is books." I bow toward the shelves, shift in my work boots. One creaks. I turn back around to find her studying me, two S lines lying on their sides across her brow.

"I wasn't planning on being a librarian," she says at last. "Life doesn't always go in the preplanned direction."

"You weren't?" I plant my elbows on the desk that runs between us and fit my chin into my hands. She's a mystery, too, this Ms. McDermott. "What happened?" I say. "I mean, if you don't mind me asking."

"Someone broke my heart," she says, simply, no details. "Books saved me, so I became a librarian."

"Just like that?"

"Well, no, Katie. Healing takes time. New directions do. It takes a long time, too, to return to yourself."

"But do you love being a librarian?"

"I do."

I nod, wishing I could ask her so much more about herself—about who broke her heart, who changed her life, if she's all through with healing, if anybody ever is, if she'll ever fall in love again. But there are some lines that shouldn't be crossed, and people's secrets are theirs alone until their secrets are set free.

"You mentioned a year?" she says now.

"Nineteen fifty-four."

"Of course," she says.

"But I have a day now, too, Ms. McDermott. A month. September 10, 1954."

"You are one heck of a spy," she says, coming toward me, high in her shoes. Her skirt makes the sound of sheets drying in the wind.

"You think you can help?"

"There are places to start," she says. "Let's go find out what we can." She heads for the microfilm room and I follow, and when we arrive, she snaps on a light, reaches high for a blue box marked MAIN LINE NOW, and slides it toward her, popping open the lid as she does. From the box she pulls a wide brown strip of film and begins to thread the film through the reader. When she presses a button, something snaps, and now pages and pages of *Main Line Now* are flashing by.

"These are ghastly things," she says, meaning the reader, which zips and moans as the film speeds through.

"Kind of scary," I agree.

"They do the trick, though, when nothing else does." As she speaks, the film edges up to 1954, and now that she's taken the century this far, she slows the reader's speed. We're through May, through June, through July and August. Ms. McDermott switches to the dial control to advance the film to September 9, 1954. A whole day goes by, and then another, and here we are: September 11.

"The day before," she says, "is revealed by the day after. At least in *Main Line Now.*" Pulling her hair from her face, she twists it all the way to one side and fits her glasses on her nose. "Well, will you look at this," she says, but I'm already all over it.

"The day of the storm," I say.

"The storm," she echoes.

"Storm like a bowling ball," I say, the old refrain.

"So what does it mean," Ms. McDermott asks, "for the case of Miss Martine?"

"I don't know. I mean, I don't know yet."

"Everything takes time," she tells me.

I nod. "I guess."

"Come and find me when you're done, okay?" She turns toward the circulation desk—all grace and style. I bet she was a dancer. Once.

The storm, as it turns out, is front-page news—as bad as Reny said it was, and maybe even worse. On the microfilm the photos are blurs; the captions are dramatic. There's a barge knocked loose on a river and smashed up with a dam. There's a field of cows up to their knees in floodwater. There are sheds flattened by the limbs of trees, a barn that caught on fire, and beside the big story are the little stories of a child being rescued by a dog, an old lady rafted on a piece of plank wood—gone a whole mile on top of the swollen-in-the-streets river.

I read for news of the Everlasts, find none, look for images of the estate, but whatever happened didn't happen there, or happened where nobody could see it or where nobody spoke of it, or where it was less important, absolutely, than the third-page story of a bound-for-Richmond train that jumped the tracks and landed in a pile that looked, from overhead, like a twisted J. FIVE DEAD, the headline reads, and with my breath held, I scan the article for the names of the deceased, find them, finally—Hauptman, Wachtner, Stentson, Long, Clancy—no Everlast there, no Miss Martine, but still I'm speeding through the pages of *Main Line Now*, so that the room grows hot with the hurried whirl of the machine, then quiets, then heats. Nothing. However and why ever Miss Martine disappeared was never answered by that paper. She is not among the dead, but also not among the living.

I let the microfilm rewind and snap it free from the

reader. Turn off the lights in this little room and go to find Ms. McDermott. I see her in the stacks across the way, helping a man find some volume. She sees me, I wave, place the film on the circulation desk. I head out the door into the heat of the day.

Chapter Twenty-one

Funny thing. My being late doesn't matter. By the time I get to the estate, the place has stilled: Old Olson has wrapped the site in caution tape and told the others to go home, and now as I hurry down the hill, Reny and Ida are hurrying up, Ida saying, "Don't even bother," and Reny saying, "Don't make like it's bad news if it's not. Free day off, Girl, is what Ida means. Full wages for vacation."

I hear them, but I don't feel the need to stop—

wave them off, keep going down, even when I hear Ida calling after me, accusing me. "All you young ones think you know so much. I say don't bother." I am close enough now to get a better look at the site, all fenced off with yellow like the scene of some crime, and to see Old Olson himself, standing with his arms crossed in a knot, talking to Danny. Owen is strapping on his backpack, which looks all-but-lunch empty to me, no more turtle shells. By the time I get to my side of the stepping-stone bridge, Owen is crossing in my direction.

"Hear the news, Girl?" he calls.

"Day off?" I say.

He puts one foot down on the first stream stone, shifts his backpack, takes another step forward. "Cool or what?"

"What's going on?"

"I don't know," he says, halfway over now. "You'd have to ask Old Olson. All he said is that Miss Martine changed her mind. No more gazebo. Tomorrow we go back to weeding."

"No more gazebo?" I repeat. "That's weird."

The straps of Owen's backpack are pulling across his lacrossy shoulders. "Sweet is what I'd call it," he says. "Except my mother has to come back and get us."

"You guys need a third car."

"You're telling me! One problemo with that scenario, Girl: My dad's the world's cheapest rich guy." He laughs. Starts digging in his pocket for his phone. "You heading up?" he asks.

"In a minute," I tell him. "Going to find out from Danny what Old Olson has to say." Across the stream Old Olson still has his big arms crossed, and I can't read Danny's face beneath his cap.

"Catch you tomorrow, then."

"Yeah. Tomorrow."

"Don't work too hard." He laughs.

"Wouldn't ever."

He bends forward a little as the hill rises beneath him. Ida and Reny are out of sight, gone.

It takes a while before Danny and Old Olson are done, and Old Olson never unties his arms. "Hey," Danny says when he sees me.

"What's up?" I ask.

"Day off."

"I heard."

"I'm thinking it's suspicious." He pulls me close and whispers something into my cap, but I can't hear, so I turn toward him, ask him with my eyes. He says he'll tell me later, and now we are walking inside the shade beside the stream—up and around the hill, gaining distance from Old Olson, Danny not talking, me just waiting. He stays close, so close, and is about to say something—I feel it—when Peter drives by in his own little cart, his hard white hat pulled down on his head like he is going on safari. When he's gone, I turn to Danny—*tell me*—but it's too late: Yvonne steps out from behind a tree, waving hello to us both. By the time we get to the entrance gates, Mrs. Santopolo has pulled up in her champagne-colored SUV, looking late for something else. Danny takes off running.

"Gotta go," he says.

I call after him. "Danny?"

"Meet me here," he says. "Tonight. Just after dark."

"Here? You're serious?" I am half whispering, half calling out loud enough for anyone who might be listening to hear.

"Do I look like I'm messing around?" And he doesn't, really, he looks like he means what he says, and also like he is glad to have walked the shade line with me.

Chapter *Twenty-two*

Riding your bike at night is not the same as riding it during the day. It's a different slice of speed, where you're up off the ground and you're cracking the shadows and the deer in the trees are frozen deer until you've passed and gone. The air is not so hot tonight. My hair is flying backward. I can't see every bump and turn, but I know this road by heart, and besides, the stars are bright and the moon is filling back in, and here I am now, banking in on Miss Martine's, braking on my silver zipper in the dark, leaving Dad in his studio with the painting that, he announced at dinner, is absolutely, no doubt about it, the John Butler Everlast rendition of through-and-through regret. Dad said that he wanted to spend more time studying it through his million pairs of glasses, and I said that was cool and that I'd come in later on, but first I wanted to take a ride around the block; wouldn't be gone long, I told him. "Be careful," he said. He didn't ask a single question, didn't even press me about my research, and maybe that's because he's still distracted but also because I'm not a daughter who has ever given him much trouble. Mom used to say that being responsible has its own rewards, and the more I live, the more I figure that she was right about that.

I'm the first one here. At least I don't see Danny, see only the one light in the one window at Miss Martine's, which I watch for a very long time. Nothing moves.

Nothing passes behind it or before it, the room doesn't change color like rooms do when there's TV, and I don't hear music, either, only the singing of the frogs down by the stream, and the crickets, and I think those are cicadas, and when I really think about it, I hear things messing around in the trees—squirrels, probably, or birds. The lights are on at Old Olson's house, but only a few lights, upstairs, and if Danny and I keep to the path near the stream, we should keep our cover. I lay my bike down in the grass beside the nearest stone post. I watch the road, looking for Danny. There are footsteps now, something in the shadows moves. My heart bangs high and hard right near my throat, and it's dark, and I'm waiting, and finally I'm thinking maybe Danny isn't coming, but now there's the sound of something, and it's Danny.

"You walked?" I ask, a hoarse whisper.

"Had to. Both my parents are out to wherever, and besides, I didn't want to have to explain." He wears long-distance sneakers, and the bill of his cap sticks out from his back jeans pocket.

"So," I say, and I wonder if he can hear my heart. When he smiles, it's like there's another moon in the sky, so bright that I worry about Old Olson, in whatever room he's sitting in, looking outside to see, and that Miss Martine, wherever she is, will notice, too. We're trespassing, and it's wrong, but I wouldn't trade this for anything.

"What's the plan?" I whisper to Danny.

"We're following a hunch," he says. He slips his arm around me, and we start walking side by side in the deepest part of the shadows, as close to the edge as we can get, as far away from the two houses as possible, until we are beside the stream, which bends. The trees overhead are dark and wild, and there are definitely squirrels out here, possibly raccoons, and the ferns look like they're caught up in some prayer, eyes closed and heads bowed. I'm listening to the birds, to the stream. I'm keeping my eye on Old Olson's house, where the same lights stay on in the same windows and no door has come flying open.

"Danny," I whisper, "where are we going?"

"Tell me you haven't already guessed," he says, pulling me closer, making me think, like I've already been thinking, how totally depressing it is that he's going to BU in two weeks. But here he is now, his arm the just-right weight across my shoulders, his hair so curly without the cap, I want to touch it. "You go the library today?" he asks.

"I did."

"You find anything?"

"Nothing much," I say. "Nothing useful." We've reached the part of the stream where the bridge cuts over, the one that's been built for the golf cart. This is the widest part of the stream right here, where the watercress is thickest and the frogs are loudest, and as we step onto the wooden slats, one rattles. Danny freezes in place, lets the echo die down. We both take a look back at Old Olson's, wait for a light to go on, a door to slam, but nothing like that happens. "We stand in the clear," Danny says.

"I can't believe we're doing this."

From the bridge I can see where the moon falls down between the big arms of a tree and floats itself on the water. It's a pale mossy color and more like an oval than a circle as it lies there not moving, but slightly moving, depending on how you see it. "The moon is with us," Danny says, and I say, "Now are you going to tell me?" Because we're still on the bridge, and we haven't gone forward. Danny takes his arm from my shoulders. I shiver a little, lean against him.

"All right," Danny says, sighing like it's going to be this really long story. I wait. I like standing this close to Danny; I like waiting. "I got here early this morning, really early, okay? Before even Old Olson was around."

"How?"

"How what?"

"How'd you get here so early?"

"My dad," Danny says, "but that's not the point. The thing is, I got to the site and I did some digging around."

"God, Danny."

"What?"

"I mean, that's taking a pretty big chance, don't you think?"

"I guess."

"Anyone could have seen you—Yvonne. Peter. Amy. Old Olson. Reny. Ida. Anybody. Miss Martine herself. Even Miss Martine." Danny's so tall that I have to lift my eyes toward his, but he's turned away, toward the stream and its floating-to-nowhere moon.

"Do you want to know what's there or not?" he asks.

"I want to know."

"Do you want to guess first?"

"I can't."

"A trunk."

"What?" I step to the side to get a better look at him, to see if he's messing with me. A slat of bridge floor creaks again. I check back at Old Olson's. Nothing. I look back at Danny, and wait. Again.

"Like I said: a trunk. Like one of those big old things you see in black-and-white movies. The kind they'd pull off of old trains and steamboats and stuff."

"An *actual* trunk?" I say, trying to figure what it could mean. I settle back closer to Danny.

"Big leather thing, from what I can tell. Sunk deep in, but definitely there. I could trace it with my fingers."

"So this dig was never about clearing a foundation for a gazebo," I say.

"Not that I can figure."

"It was about digging out a trunk. Using a little

hired muscle to get back to some buried chunk of past."

"That's what I'm thinking."

I picture the thing buried in the dirt like that, imagine Danny tracing it around with his fingers. What could be inside? Jewelry? Furs? Bars of gold? A dead person? What could Old Olson want with it, or Miss Martine?

"So that's my news," Danny says, pulling me closer than I have ever been to him, ever been to any boy. I tilt my chin, and he's looking straight down at me—a clear shot into my soul. I try to swallow, but now my heart's high in my throat, beating hard and furious as the wings on that strange, crack-of-dawn finch. Danny smooths the bangs from my face. "Katie," he says, and do you know how different that is from calling me Girl, from calling me any other thing? "How come you were never in any of my classes? How did I miss out on you?"

"I've been taking too many A.P.s, I guess." I smile.

He laughs. "Yeah. You're such a loser." He keeps looking at me.

"You're going away," I say. "To BU, in two weeks."

"I guess I am."

"That totally sucks."

"I guess it does."

"I hate good-byes." I feel like I'm going to cry, and how stupid is that?

"Two weeks is fourteen days," Danny says, pulling me even closer toward him.

"Yeah, but it still sucks."

He takes his arm from across my shoulder. He reaches for my hands instead, and his hands are big, his thumbs are worked and rough, his hands feel right on my hands. When he bends, I stand tall and we meet in one sweet kiss. Danny Santopolo has kissed plenty of times, I can tell. He makes this one kiss last forever, until it's me who falls back down to my real height.

"Cool moon," he says finally, looking out on the

stream, his arm settled back now on my shoulders.

"Yeah." My finch heart beats. I can't say more.

He places my hand in his hand, pulls it up to his lips. "You want to see the trunk for yourself?"

Chapter Twenty-three

The lights are still on when I steer my bike right past Sammy Mack's drive onto my own. Dad's got the studio blazing, lit up like a fire. Two pairs of glasses sit on the slope of his nose. It's close to eleven, and he doesn't look up when I tap on the door, doesn't turn when I say hello. I feel like I've been gone for years—my head somewhere that my body's not.

"Hey," I say.

"Hey, kiddo." He doesn't turn. "You have a good ride?"

"Uh-huh." I straighten my bangs with my fingertips, take a swallow of air to help calm my heart. Danny's out there somewhere walking home, and there's a trunk buried deep at Miss Martine's—a trunk, I saw for myself. Danny put his hand on my hand, helped me trace its outline in the dark. "I asked Old Olson what it was," Danny told me. "He wouldn't admit it was there."

"You ready for news?" Dad asks now, his question bringing me back.

"Sure," I say. "I'm ready."

"You're not seeming all that excited."

"Long bike ride," I say. "Sorry." I cross over toward him, weave between all the lights, stand by the stool where he sits before the Everlast canvas. He's got his kit of pigments at his feet, a coffee can of brushes on the black ledge of a nearby easel. Dad would make the perfect mad scientist in any casting call. "Seriously," I say. "What's up?"

"In the John Butler Everlast version of regret, we have ourselves a blackened city, and we have ourselves a garden," Dad says, sweeping his arms around in front of the canvas in his weird way of pointing things out. He looks at me, and I give him a nod. "This," he says, "you have already seen for yourself."

"That is a fact. I have."

"And in that garden there is light. Bright greens, bright yellows, bright pinks. This, too, you've already noted." He sounds like a magician about to pull a cloth from a cage of doves.

"Got it."

"But what else do you suppose we discover in that garden?"

A trunk? I want to say, but I wouldn't even know how to start to tell that story. "Don't know."

He takes the first pair of glasses off his nose and

pushes them down on my own. Everything in the room looks ten times bigger. I feel a little seasick. "A shell," I say finally, because I see it now—hardly there but certainly there. A turtle shell hung on the base of a wide tree, just below where the first branch twists out and upward. "The shell I told you about."

"The guy sure had a vision," Dad says.

"Yeah," I say, and I feel my heart going at it again. I'm thinking about Owen's prize, thinking about Danny's kiss, thinking about the bridge, the trunk, the dark, Miss Martine and her one-light house, Old Olson all silent and denying. The storm and the day of the storm.

"Would have loved to have been in on one of Everlast's board meetings," Dad goes on. "They must have been unique."

"What do you mean?"

"Well, I took a little trip today."

"You did?"

"Is my life so boring that a little trip is so exciting?"

"Sorry."

"Just down the road, to Quality Chemicals," he continues. "They let me into their archives."

"That's cool."

"You want the long and the short of it?"

"Sure."

"John Butler Everlast took a leave of absence at the very height of his success. Left the company in the hands of his chief financial officer, which wasn't, as it turned out, a good thing for Quality."

"When was that?"

"The leave? Well, funny thing. September 1954, it started. He stayed away a full year afterward."

"Do the records say why he left?" I press.

"Family matter is what the records say."

"No kidding," I say.

"Right. Like we didn't have that much already figured for ourselves."

"So put it all together, and what do you get?" I ask, taking off his pair of magnifiers and passing them back, stumbling around in my own head to fit every clue together.

"Don't have the full skinny on this one yet, Miss D'Amore. I restore art. This painting needs a bona fide detective."

"I guess," I say, looking back over the canvas again—the blackened city, the lit-up garden. Miss Martine has to be somewhere in the painting. I just don't know where, and maybe it's hard to know why it matters, except: A woman has gone missing for fifty-three whole years. That's more than three of my lifetimes. And if I know where she is, maybe it will be easier to find my mother, or some way of living, of moving forward though she's gone.

Dad catches his whole chin in his big hand and shakes his head. "Did you enjoy your bike ride?" he asks.

"Didn't you already ask me that?"

"Perhaps, but I'm forgetting what you said."

"I said I did, and thank you very much."

"The D'Amores don't do sarcasm," he says, and I laugh.

"Going to bed, Dad," I say, kissing him on the head, weaving back through the lights toward the dark.

"Hey, Katie," he says when I reach the door.

"Yeah?"

"I almost forgot. A Ms. McDermott showed up here earlier. Left a package for you by the front-door step."

"Ms. *McDermott*?" I ask, turning back to see if he's messing with me.

"Would I lie," he says, "about that?"

"Ms. McDermott, the fabulous librarian?"

"Well, she was pretty fabulous," Dad admits. "And she did mention something about research."

Chapter *Twenty-four*

The moon is gigantic—a big white throb in a blue-black sky. Ms. McDermott's package is propped up against the door, with just my name on it—KATIE— and her initials: A.M. There's hardly any weight to it, feels like it could have been blown away by a fraction of a wind, but it's just so still tonight. I sit on the stoop wishing Danny were still near, his arm around me, his laugh, because when I open whatever Ms. McDermott has dropped off, I'm going to need another kiss.

The envelope isn't sealed, and something flimsy falls right out into my lap—a photograph, size of my hand. It's a slick black-and-white on one side. A handwritten note on the other, blue ink. *Miss Martine Everlast. May 1954*, the note says. Miss Martine, the same year that she vanished.

I turn the photo faceup and lift it higher, toward the moon. She isn't glamour here, not the star of some ball, not wearing diamonds in her hair, which falls long and dark, past the bottom edge of the photograph. Her blouse is hardly a blouse, more like a shirt, something a man might have worn, with a stiff, starched collar, and now I need better light to see her. But I also need to sit right here and think, while Dad works his painting across the drive, and Sammy trampolines his way to bed across the street, and Jessie and Ellen are out being best friends, and Danny is or isn't home quite yet. History is never absolute truth, Ms. McDermott said, and

I don't feel in danger of drawing wrong conclusions here, but I don't even have a single guess at how all this adds up. I have these clues and no theory, and when I stare at the moon, it's only one unblinking eye, staring straight back. Add a recluse to a garden to a very odd Old Olson. Add a hole, a turtle, a trunk, a painting about regret, a day in a year—I'd rather do calculus. It's as silent out here as it is inside all the rooms of the house, which are so pitch-dark and so ridiculously big. I'm tired, too tired to stay here on the step with my thoughts swimming in circles.

"Night, Dad," I say, but not loud enough for him to hear me.

"Night, Mom." But never loud enough, and now as I sit on this stoop another time comes tumbling back, another place—Cascais—which is where we traveled to after we'd traveled through Barcelona, Mom saying, "Our vacation can't be finished yet," Mom making the calls to delay our flight home and to get us to this town in Portugal. "It's only a few more days, Jimmy," she told my dad. "And we're so close, and besides, when will we get to Europe again?" Our clothes were end-of-trip dirty, and I was missing Ellen and Jessie, but Dad said, "If you want to see Cascais, we will. But after that, Claire, we really will have to get ourselves home."

"Summer's supposed to be sweet in Portugal," Mom said, kissing Dad hard on the lips and hugging me.

But when we got there, the weather was wild. It was like a mist had been tossed off from the distant hills of Sintra—a rolling mist, which grew more dense and more insistent once it reached the streets of Cascais, and which carried inside it a big, chilled wind. By dusk on the first day we were all wishing for the sweaters we didn't have, and by evening Dad and I didn't want to leave the hotel. "Room service," Dad practically pleaded. "It'll be fun."

But Mom had seen a restaurant with a terrace sitting up above the town, and she had set her heart on it.

"I want to watch the sea," she said, "at night." And so that's where we went—to the terrace above the town, ordering pizzas with strange things on them and sitting on our napkins so the wind wouldn't steal them away. We could hardly hear each other talk because of the wind, and the truth is, Mom didn't seem like she was up for that much talking, so we sat. Across the way we could see the lip of the Atlantic, the fishing boats, the tourists being blown about. On the terrace, the wind kicked at our ankles and flapped the tablecloth against our knees, and toward the end of our meal the open umbrella beside ours snapped right off its metal stand and pirouetted into our table, tossing the knives and the forks and the pizza plates down, spilling a bottle of wine.

"I'm thinking we'll have dessert to go," Dad said. "We can watch the sea from the hotel." But Mom was turned toward the harbor, where a crowd had begun to gather, and she wasn't going back to the hotel.

"There's going to be a parade," she told us.

"In this weather?" Dad said.

"Look," she said. "How beautifully strange."

I watched then, and Dad did, as the crowd by the harbor swelled and some sort of music began, music we could hear from where we sat because of the direction of the wind. "A parade," Mom said again, and after Dad paid, neither one of us asked or protested, we just followed Mom out of the terrace and down the hill—Dad putting his arm around Mom to keep her warm and to protect her from the toddlers, children, grown-ups, tourists—all of us heading to the shore. I walked behind them. I walked beside them. I walked backward when the wind blew hard, and when I turned around, the parade was right there; it took us in.

The parade was all these little kids. It was girls fighting the wind in their big, strange hats and flaring dresses—green, I remember, white and red. It was boys in suspendered pants and their own strange hats, who pushed wooden wheelbarrows before them. The weird thing about the wheelbarrows was how they were laced with rods of light—orange, rose, and green light rods that were bent to look like flowers—and how at the same one moment the boys lifted their wheelbarrows to the sky, like signs. That's when the girls began to skip and spin, and then it was like standing inside a merry-go-round, like whirling with the merry-go-round. All that color and light was going up and down to the strangest sort of music, while the wind blew in from the sea.

I lost Dad that night, but not for long. I lost Mom until the parade moved on, wound itself away from the harbor and up into the crooked streets. I turned and saw her standing on the edge of things—too thin, I realize now, and frail, the wind caught up in her hair. She'd kept her secret the whole trip long. She stood in that strange, chilled mist, alone, alive, but knowing what would come. History is never absolute truth. It isn't just the thing that was. It's the thing that could have been.

Chapter *Twenty-five*

I wake with the photograph here beside me, on my pillow—the finch doing kamikaze against my bedroom window. It does its hammering thing and its flying away thing, and this time I know where it's going. This time I remember Sammy Mack's finger, pointing straight to my parents' bedroom window.

"All right," I say. "I'm coming." Placing my feet onto the floor, pulling my bathrobe on, slipping the photo of Miss Martine into the bathrobe pocket. It's early, before dawn. I hear the TV mumble-blaring downstairs. Dad must have come in late, turned it on, fallen asleep to its noise, and he can't hear me now, won't hear me standing outside his own bedroom door. In this house, you can break the locks just by applying the right pressure—by holding the knob up, pulling the door toward the hall, then pressing the knob back down. The locks in this house don't mean a thing. They're just signs: DO NOT ENTER HERE.

But I'm going in because the finch says to, because I miss my mother, because I need her, because maybe just being around the things that she loved will bring me some kind of answers. After a while, the lock breaks free. Gently I tap against the door, and it opens, and then it opens more. Everything but Mom is here. Everything, the way she lived it.

I close the door behind me, fast, so that not one bit of Claire D'Amore escapes. I jiggle the knob. I stand and take her in: Her favorite perfume, her straw hats. The photographs that always hung still hanging, all smoky with dust, and if I opened her closet and her bureau drawers, I'd find the things she loved to wear and the things she bought but never wore, dresses with their tags still on.

Along the windowsills are the tinted bottles, and beyond the windows is the glow of sun, the colors of early day. Mom and Dad slept in a queen-sized bed, with three pillows on Dad's side and one on Mom's, until Mom got sick and Dad propped her up with all four, except for the end, when Mom said, "I need to sleep, Jimmy," and Dad helped her lie flat. Mom's side was the window side. She liked the windows open, even in winter, piling the blankets high on freezing nights and saying to Dad, when he begged her to shut them, "But it's so exhilarating, Jimmy. It's just like camping." I'd hear them laughing from down the hall. No one in our house watched Letterman when my mother was alive.

The sun continues to rise. Outside, the sky grows more yellow-blue, and inside, the shadows are smoking away, and all I want is to be with my mother, to hear her explain to me why it was that she had to go, how it makes sense, or is even in the neighborhood of fair, how she kept her dying such a secret. Why a secret? I'm taking all these A.P. courses, but none of them have explained vanishing. None of them say how it is that a talk-of-the-town woman disappears after a storm, or how a mother who opens her arms to your best friends, to everything, can slip away to a place that you can't find. Was her living so well in Barcelona a lie, or was it her gift to Dad and to me? Was Cascais ecstasy, or a warning?

The last thing my father did before he shut this door for good was put everything back to the way it was before Mom got cancer. Every shoe in the shoe bag. Every drawer on its runner. Every dress on its hanger. Every hat on its hook. He piled the pillows back the way they'd been and swept the floor, and now the dusty floorboards creak and snap beneath my footsteps. I sit on my mother's side of the bed. I lie down the way she once did. I fit my head into where her head used to fit inside her pillow. I would give all I ever learned or thought I knew to hear her say my name. "Ask me anything, Mom," I say. "I'll even tell you about Danny." I close my eyes to hear her or to dream her back, but ghosts, I've figured out this much, don't work that way. What I see in my mind is the last time my mother saw me—her face nothing but eyes by then, her hands so thin and so pale.

"You make me proud, Katie," she said.

I said, "I do?"

"Everything about you, love."

"Mom?" I said. "Mom, don't leave me?"

"I'm not going far," she said. "You'll find me." Then she closed her eyes, and she didn't open them again, except once, when Dad was back sitting in his chair, and the room was full and ripe with color.

Dad locked their room to keep her in. I've broken back in to find her.

When I open my eyes, parts of the sun have found parts of the bottles, and fuzzy sprays of rose, peach, violet, and lemon have been tossed against the far wall. My mother used to call this kind of color suggested color, and as I lie watching, I remember her lying here saying, "It's a brand-new show every day." For her that was the best part, how the color show was never the same, just like the best part of Dad, she thought, was that he was always doing something goofy, though she preferred to say "surprising." "He has reinvented the male species," she'd tell me when we were folding the warm towels in the laundry room, or spooning the last of the brownie batter into a tray, or weeding out her garden, or stringing lights around the branches of her last Christmas tree, which we put up early every

November, because she loved Christmas best of all. "There's nobody like Jimmy D'Amore."

But there was nobody like Mom, either, and if she were here, she'd tell me something about how red is always chasing yellow. I'll never have another new Mom story. I only have the old ones to keep, which is why I have stayed so quiet since she passed, why I've been keeping to myself, because if I talk, if I say too much about Mom, I'm thinking that the parts I still have will escape, like bubbles.

I wonder again what she'd have made of Miss Martine and the gazebo mystery—of Old Olson asking us to dig to a trunk he hoped we'd never see. His was a stupid plan, but he went ahead with it, and that could mean only one thing: He was desperate to get to the trunk, willing to take some risks. Something has happened after all these years to give that trunk new meaning, and even though you could say that it's none of my business, it's come to matter to me. It's a problem

I have a shot at solving, a question I have to answer.

I slip the photo of Miss Martine out of my bathrobe pocket. In the morning glow of my parents' room, I stare at it and let it stare straight back at me. There's more to see by the light of day than there was last night on the stoop—loose, long curls in Miss Martine's hair, a pin clipped to the edge of her shirt collar that looks something like a turtle—yes, a turtle—and there, in the crook of her arm, a single long-stemmed flower: fleur-de-lis. There's the bark of a big, old tree in the background, and a little bit of sky to the side, just enough to get a feeling for some sun. But there's something, too, in the way that Miss Martine looks so hard at me, something in her flinty eyes that I'm starting to think is familiar.

Really, truly, freaky familiar.

I close my eyes. Try to dream my way toward a knowing, try to conjure Mom and her wisdom. The kaleidoscopic colors pulse, hash, jumble—it's practically a noise they make. The sun pushes in from beyond—whisked heat. I imagine Miss Martine in her house alone, imprisoned by the darkness that descended on her garden, by the years that passed without her really living them. Vanished. Vanquished? Escape or rescue? A turtle's shell, those fleurs-de-lis—all varnish, no color, no light. Something got stolen in the midst of paradise. A father took a stance and lived with sorrow. A daughter withered. My mother died too soon inside the exuberance of color. Miss Martine has lived a life set apart, for too long.

I feel a tear begin to leak down my cheek. I am, all of a sudden, immensely tired. I long to stop walking around with all these questions.

In the absolute silence of this room, time goes on without me. Runs through me and past. When I open my eyes again, it's to the sound of frisk and clatter, to that finch, outside my mother's window, tapping its beak on the glass.

"You again." I sigh. "You're kind of amazing. For a bird." Lying in my mother's bed, not moving, I watch the thing flit and flutter, bang, bop, plunge, return, punch its ballet into the glass. The finch looks past its beak, through the window, through the streams of color. It plays its game a dozen times until reluctantly, slowly, I lift myself off the bed, plant my feet on the floor, step toward the window and the sill of colored bottles. I arrive, and the finch disappears, and all I have before me now is sky and gravel and, to the left, below, my mother's garden. The yellow, white, and red of the big fat dahlias. The effusive zinnias. The catmint and the mounds of hellebores that survived the winter and bloomed in spring and sit there making their plans for next season. Everything that could have bloomed without Mom's help has, miraculously, bloomed, even things that aren't supposed to survive the frost. Even the weeds that have wedged into all the empty spaces can't contradict my mother's beauty, or her idea of beauty, or the need for beauty to live on. "I'm not going far," she said.

Throwing the window latch, I push my weight against the glass, and though it takes an extra urging, it finally gives. Fitting my fingers inside the contraptions of the screen window, I free that, too. Nothing separates me now from the world outside, and I lean out as far as I can into summer—look forward, look down, upon Mom's garden. I stand here making promises to myself—a daughter's promises: to live my life with my eyes wide open. To honor exuberance, and color.

Somewhere down the road, I think, Miss Martine is standing—above a dream, above a garden, above a story. She's standing there alone, except for Old Olson, who is alone in his own kind of way. I think about the two of them now, walled off in that place. The two of them overseeing the seasons but never going far beyond their gates. All of a sudden, something falls into place. The portrait. Those eyes. A connection. Because Miss

Martine's eyes are Old Olson's eyes. There can be no two ways about it.

"Jesus," I say, and pull my head back through the window, to this side of my mother's room, where now the before is mixed up with the after, where suddenly Miss Martine isn't just some old recluse; she is somebody's mother. I notice a fluttering near a tree beyond. The gold breast of the bright finch, winging off.

Chapter Twenty-six

I don't even bother with a shower. I pull on yesterday's clothes, stuff my hair into Danny's BU cap, tie on my shoes, and hurry down the wide stairs past the photographs and the restored portraits, straight into the kitchen.

"Howdy, stranger," Dad says when he turns around and I'm there. "Old Olson give you another paid day off?"

"Dad," I say, "I'm kind of late. I'm sorry." I start

throwing lunch things into my backpack, pick up a banana for the road, stuff a couple extra-big plastic bags into the backpack, hoist the backpack. I head into the mudroom for a silver trowel and tuck that in with the rest of my stuff.

"You say hello to our guest?" Dad asks. He looks startled, maybe, by my hurry. Like he doesn't know what questions to ask.

"Hey, Sammy," I say, "what's up?" The kid has on his Spider-Man suit with the rubber mask flipped up. Two doughnuts sit on his plate beside a log of sausage that's got a stripe of burn down its long side. He is looking like he lives here, and right now, for Dad's sake, I'm glad he does.

"Jimmy and I are busy," Sammy informs me, nodding furiously and hoisting the sausage with his fingers.

"Is that a fact?" I zipper my backpack, stoop down to tie the laces of my muddy work boots, stand,

and walk toward the door.

"You're not thinking about leaving here without some breakfast?" Dad asks me. "Are you?"

"Got to, Dad." I kiss his forehead. "But I'll be back, I promise. I have something to tell you, but first there's something to do."

"Our mystery?"

I nod. "Home by seven."

"See that?" I hear him say as I step one foot out the door. "Another superhero, Sammy. This neighborhood is chock-full."

Chapter *Twenty-seven*

At Miss Martine's I walk my bike across the macadam and toward the shelter of the shed, then head back to the top of the hill and look out—see Yvonne near the top of the hill staking dahlias and Peter down by the ferns. Way on the other side from me, Amy looks like she's thinking of climbing into a tree; Owen's beside her, big green buckets in his hands. I don't see Danny, don't see Old Olson either, but where the hill stops altogether and the angle flattens and starts easing toward the stream, I see Ida and Reny, knee-deep in prairie-drop seed. Beyond them the caution tape is still on yellow fire, but there's no hole—just a lumpy recession where the hole used to be.

I don't turn toward the stream. I turn, instead, toward the house, the windows of which are lit up on one side by sun. Nothing stirs, and I head off in the house's direction, my backpack heavy, my work boots sinking into the earth of the hill. When I get to the front of the house I weave around, toward the back, alongside the porch, near the patch of pachysandra that I crunched what seems like forever ago. There are broken brown leaves that no one's replaced. There's a chance to make a small thing right.

Above me, the curtains in that same one room move, touched by the breeze. Nothing else. The only late-summer yellow in Mom's garden is the thread-leaved coreopsis, which isn't fleur-de-lis by any stretch, but it's a flag of blooming something, and now I pull them, these clumps of my mother's flowers, from the plastic bags into which I planted them this morning—six clumps drawn up while Dad and Sammy had breakfast. There are earthworms from this morning's dig in a squirm among the roots. There is the sweet deep chocolate of earth, mud worked into my fingernails. I dig out the crushed pachysandra. I edge in the yellow. The shadows change, and the day's heat rises. My mother's flowers stretch toward the sun.

I run into Ida and Reny on my way back down the hill. "You're getting yourself a late habit, aren't you, Girl?" says Ida when she sees me.

"Do you have a second?" I ask her, and she snorts.

"A second? As if we haven't already given you more than that. Go on and ask. We'll see."

"Fess up." Reny nods. He smiles his crooked-tooth smile. He claps his gloved-up hand onto my shoulder. "We're all ears."

"How long have you two been with Miss Martine?" I ask. "If you don't mind telling, that is."

Ida watches a dragonfly settle, does the math in her head, gives me an odd little look. "Right about forever," she decides.

"Before Old Olson was Old Olson," Reny adds. "At least."

"I'm thinking we showed up here in seventy-four," Ida continues, her whole face screwed into one big estimating wrinkle. "That about right, Reny? Left the Blue Hills, came this way. Long silver train with the windows down, dumped us off at Thirtieth Street Station. We were just married. We didn't know much of anything."

"Want ad," Reny says. "We were responding. Back then Old Olson was still a kid, maybe twenty. Most educated man I ever knew of, the autodidact version. Man would go around the garden citing Shakespeare, Descartes, Pascal, Mr. T. S. Eliot himself. You ever hear of T. S. Eliot?"

"Girl ain't stupid," Ida says.

"Wasn't implying," Reny answers.

"Where'd he come from?" I ask.

"Who?"

"Old Olson."

"Well, from the womb, I guess," Ida says. "I don't know. He was the gardener. He needed help. We didn't ask questions."

"We came to work," Reny says. "He kept to himself."

"And always lived in the caretaker's house?" I ask.

"What's that?" Ida says quickly, crossing her wide arms across her wide chest and staring at me hard, daring me to ask one further question. I fix the cap on my head and try to look like I haven't noticed. I study her. I study Reny. They know something, and they're not telling.

"Old Olson. He's always lived here? In that house?"

"Far back as we've known him," Reny says.

"And that's all we know," Ida says, poking Reny in the shoulder. Subtle she's not.

He turns around, takes a long look at her wrinkled face, and turns back around to me. "Yup." He nods. "About the whole length of our story."

"Why are you asking, anyway?" Ida demands.

"Just curious," I tell her.

"Curious doesn't do much for a garden," she says. "Gardens are hard work and water. Dirt, some seeds. They don't take a single benefit from people standing around talking."

"Sorry."

"Keep your smarts to your schoolwork," Ida says. "You'll be better off in the end."

I find Danny and Old Olson on the bridge above the watercress stream. A whole flock of white butterflies has lifted off just a little down breeze, and when all those white wings reach the bridge, they split off into fractions—some going under, on the stream's side, and some rising above, skimming Danny's shoulders, then rising into the shadows, toward the higher branches of the trees. Old Olson turns to watch, swiping the hat from his head. Danny turns, and the two of them stand there not seeing me, not talking to each other, just letting the wings go by. Time messes with the truth. Time puts cracks in things.

Old Olson's seen a million pairs of wings, I'm thinking, and every scrap of moon and everything that's died and everything that's grown and everything that's died again, because that's what happens in a garden; and in gardens, secrets happen, too. The hole isn't the hole anymore. Danny is leaving in thirteen days. I haven't seen Jessie or Ellen all summer. Ms. McDermott found a photograph, and in the photograph I found what I am sure is at least one truth in a pair of eyes.

But I don't know what is hidden in that trunk,

or why it matters now to Miss Martine, who disappeared some fifty years ago, but not like my mom disappeared.

What's in that trunk? I wonder

And why did Old Olson never choose to leave, to live beyond the garden?

Standing here, there's nothing I can know for absolute, hard fact except that summer's ending and senior year's about to begin, and afterward I'm going to college, and Dad will be there in that too-big house, cooking his too-big meals, staying up too late in the night, leaving two chairs empty, one for me and one for Mom, one flower in the bud vase on the table. How will I know if he'll be okay? How can I stop the things that are left from vanishing?

There's a tree casting out big skirts of shade. I go to rest my back against it.

Chapter Twenty-eight

There's one more box of Local Lore, and that's where I'm headed—to the library. It's cool as a cave down here, and with the lights off it could be any time of day. I didn't see Ms. McDermott when I pushed through the front door, didn't pass her on the steps coming down, haven't seen a soul in this basement. It's me and me only, with box number seven. I jiggle the lid loose and all the old smells rise up—the yesterday smells, the trapped scrapbook smells, the smell of tarnish. Down there in the mix I find a sweet velvet box. The pink diamond, I think, eager and nervous, but the velvet box is empty.

Beneath the box lies a folded scarf, and beneath the scarf a crusted jar of ink, and there are envelopes here, never addressed and never sent, a Montblanc pen. A leather change purse is a strange aquamarine color, but there is nothing to it, nothing inside. There's a map and an old train schedule, and way at the bottom of the box a little brown book with boxy gold letters stamped across the front: *Great Expectations*. The book's cover is soft as an old Bible's, and the pages inside are onionskin, rough and translucent at the same time. I flip to the middle before I thumb to the start, where the margins of Dickens's novel are blued with the most immaculate handwriting, miniature cursive that I have to squint to read, and sometimes between the pages there are ribbons, newsprint scraps, squashed rosebuds, little dabs of painted color, tinted flower sketches, and now:

another photograph, square with worn edges.

It's a fuzzy image—incredible fade—and on the very bottom someone has written a date in blue ink: May 20, 1954. The image itself is of a girl on horseback—Miss Martine, I'm sure of it, for those are her eyes looking out from under that cap; that is her hair streaming down; that is a clump of iris in the crook of her arm. Down on the ground is a man, maybe mid-twenties, stroking the nose of the horse and looking into the face of Miss Martine. I flip the photo to the back, and in the same blue ink is a line that reads *Olson and me, Large Junior Hunter Blue Ribbon Win, Dixon Oval, Devon Horse Show.*

Olson and me. My heart leaps up into my throat and flips and twists like it's trying to wing free, and now I turn the photo faceup again and study the man on the ground, the man with Miss Martine, whose chiseled-out jaw is the same jaw I've seen in the garden. It's the shoulders that aren't the same, the build of the body, the equestrian frame. You can always tell two people in love. This is Miss Martine, and her lover. This is Miss Martine, and her fleurs-de-lis. Her way out. Her escape. It is late May 1954. She is still alive in the world.

I thrust the lid back on the box, keep the photo with me. I hurry from the room and up the steps, and out onto the main floor of the library, where Ms. McDermott is at the Xerox machine, copying pages from some huge encyclopedia. Her turquoise blouse has its own stitched belt. She wears an immaculate white skirt, a pair of silver sandals, purple toenail polish.

"Hey," I say, and she turns, and I say "Hey" again, and she says, "What's up?" and I tell her I've found something, a photo, another date, a name. "Do you still have that microfilm handy?" I ask her. "*Main Line Now*, 1954?"

"Easily found," she says.

"Do you have a minute to help me?"

"Of course." And she leaves the encyclopedia right where it is, facedown on the copier glass. She disappears, returns with the cassette box in one hand, and now I'm hurrying beside her to the reader. "What are we looking for?" she asks me.

"May twentieth," I say. "The Devon Horse Show. Large Junior Hunter Division. A guy named Olson."

"First name or last name?"

"Don't know that."

"What *do* you know?"

"This," I say, producing the photo.

"Oh my goodness," she says, taking it in for a long time. And then she sighs, and I know that whatever sadness she feels is not just about the girl and her horseman. It's about love and what can happen to it, about what she too has lost.

It feels like a long time passes before I release the film from its reader and return it to Ms. McDermott, who sits at the circulation desk and watches me approach—her eyebrows up, her eyes full of questions. "Well?" she asks, and I say, "His name was Olson. A first name, not a last name. His last name was Long."

"Long," she repeats.

"He trained horses at Geringer's," I tell her. "He trained riders. There was a whole special feature on him in *Main Line Now*, and a little picture of him together with a student."

"Miss Martine?" she asks.

"The same," I say. I show her the photograph that had been tucked inside the book, a portrait, a true portrait, taken on the same day as the *Main Line Now* snapshot.

"So they were student and instructor."

"Yes."

"And perhaps lovers."

"Had to have been."

"And she was carrying the fleurs-de-lis in her arms?"

"Escape," I say. "That was her plan. That's what she was going for. At least, that's what I'm guessing."

I feel my eyes go hot and teary; I try to stifle a sob deep in my chest. I don't know why this makes me so sad, but it does, and the cool thing about Ms. McDermott is that she understands. She comes around to my side of the desk and puts her arm around me.

"Sometimes life just isn't fair," she says.

"She was just my age," I say.

"Yes."

"And she was going to have a baby."

"How do you know that?"

"Because of the gardener," I say. "His eyes belong to Miss Martine. His name, his jaw, belong to the horse guy."

She looks at me without saying anything, then squeezes the knob of my shoulder with her hand. "So she was a young mother," she says.

"Without a husband," I say. One tear makes its way down my cheek. I turn to look up into Ms. McDermott's face, which has become, for that one moment, a complicated and raw place. "I still don't know what we're digging for," I finally say. "I mean, at the estate."

"Sometimes you just have to ask, you know. Ask Old Olson."

"I guess that's right."

"Sometimes the truth is right there, within reach."

I nod. I feel glued to the floor in my heavy boots, incapable of going forward.

"You all right, Katie?"

"I don't know. I mean, Miss Martine's story was here all along," I say, speaking slowly, which is the only way I've ever had of stoppering my tears. "It was just all broken up, in pieces."

"Well," she says, "most of our stories are."

"I should have been able to guess," I say, brushing my hand beneath my eye. "At least at something. It all seems so obvious now. Well. Sort of. And, like, I haven't even been that nice to Old Olson. I haven't even thought that maybe he had something sad to hide."

"Guessing would have meant jumping straight to conclusions."

"No fun in that, you said."

"No purpose."

"Maybe."

"Katie?"

"Yes?"

"Your mother would be proud."

"Of what?"

"Of you. Working things through. Working them out."

It's really odd, how Ms. McDermott does this, I think. Like she's channeling my mom.

"Don't be a stranger."

"I won't. I promise."

"Libraries would be empty without people like you."

"They'd still be full of books," I say.

"Books don't make a bit of difference, unless somebody reads them searching for something." She smiles her perfect Fifth Avenue smile. Whoever broke her heart was a loser.

"See you around," I say.

"Yes, you will," she answers. I wave over my shoulder, push through the door, head down the steps, and unlock my bike from the stand. I steer past the parking lot and down the first hill, and now I'm flying past the new and the old, the vanished and the resurrected, the surviving herd of cows, the stream. I should get home, I know I should, but something steers me the other way, until I am back at Miss Martine's. An hour from now, night will fall, and already Dad will be wondering where I am. But sometimes you just have to break the rules.

The shadows are deep; all is silent. I roll my bike down the macadam and toward the big house on the hill. I stop and take a long look at every single window. There's silence, everywhere—upon the hill and in the shadows. There's silence, and somewhere in the silence is Old Olson. I leave my bike where it is, head down the hill.

Chapter Twenty-nine

I find him staking dahlias against his own little caretaker's house. His hat off and his shirtsleeves rolled, most of his face in the shadows. He seems younger to me than he has before—less hard edged and maybe more lonesome—and I'm near enough to the stream to hear the water running through, its movement over rocks, so that it isn't so silent right here where he works.

I shouldn't be here, I know, by myself, near dark.

If he knew, my dad would not be pleased; Danny either. Danny would say I've gone too far, that some risks should not be taken. But I am here to see this thing through, and I don't feel frightened.

I wait until he sees me. I stand here leaning against an old birch tree, watching him work, watching the gold eyes of a rabbit glow from beneath a holly bush, eyeing all the stuff that's grown up between his house and the estate—the hedges, the trellis, the passion-flowers laced through the trellis. The dahlias have peaked and their faces are heavy—big, rust-colored accordion-fold faces that are too heavy for their stems. He props each bloom back up by force of a meshy metal cage. He steps back to look at the whole, and then he turns, and that's when he sees me. His back goes straight as a rod; his shoulders hunch.

"Katie," he says. That's all. He pulls the gloves off his hands—the right one, the left—and drops them. He fits a pair of garden shears into the pocket of his pants.

"Forget something?" He just stands there, daring me to explain myself. That gold-eyed rabbit comes flying out from beneath the bush. Scuttles in the air between us, then past me, is gone into the woods.

"I found something," I tell him, for it seems the best way to start.

"You found what?" He clips his words, uses as few as possible.

"I mean, in the library. In a box. Inside a book. *Great Expectations.*"

He levels me with a long stare. "You always did strike me as the bookish type," he says. He puts a hand around his chin, which he scratches slowly, as if there's no real itch. It gets so quiet between the two of us that all I can hear is the stream beyond, the buzz of a bug, a stick breaking somewhere in the woods. Squirrels, I think. Or that rabbit.

"It's a photograph," I tell him. "A picture I think you should have."

He drops his hand. His brow goes crinkly. He doesn't move or say a word, just stares at me with those flinty eyes. I step toward him, reach into my bag, and retrieve the image. I balance it on my palm, stretch my hand toward him. He still won't move. He watches my face first, and then my hand, studies my eyes again, finally leans forward. Leans and lifts the photo from my hand and balances it on his own palm. I want him to say something, one thing, but he does not.

"May 1954," I tell him, because night has started to come on in a hurry and maybe it's too dark now for him to read the tiny blue words. "The Devon Horse Show. Your mom. She won the blue ribbon."

He looks from the photograph to me, and back down to the photo, and from a branch somewhere high above, a blackbird screams. I hear the scramble of the rabbit beneath bushes close to the stream, the running around of squirrels, another bird. "Where did you find this?" he finally demands.

I tell him again. "Inside a book. Inside a box. At the library."

He turns and stands that way—his back to me, his body in the shadows, his shoulders shifting down, his head bending toward the photo. "It just seemed like you should have it," I tell him, because he won't talk and somebody has to. "There are these boxes," I start again. "Seven of them at the library, and I've been sorting through them. I've been trying to understand."

"Understand what?"

"This place. Miss Martine. The dig. Things that disappear. People."

"Seems more like spying."

"The boxes are anyone's to sort through. Local Lore. They just arrived one day—stacked outside near the book-return slot when Ms. McDermott got to work. They needed cataloging, and I volunteered. I mean, I'd started working for Miss Martine, and then there was that turtle shell, you know, the one that Owen found, and it had that indentation inside, and then my dad, at home, has been working on a painting—he restores paintings, that's what he does—and it's an Everlast painting, as it turns out, and I don't know: I wanted to understand."

It's a long speech, and it gets his attention. He turns and faces me, and his eyes are brisk and bright though his face is muted by shadows, and he doesn't look mad, doesn't even seem confused. More like he seems relieved. "Miranda Everlast Thomas." That's what he says.

"Excuse me?" He has said the name softly. I step closer.

"My mother's cousin," he says. "She died a couple months ago. Her son's been cleaning out her house, readying it for a sale. Or so I've heard. We're not personally in touch, and from what I understand, he was rather estranged from his mom."

I shake my head, bewildered.

"She was my mother's best friend, too," he explains, "besides being her cousin. My mother trusted her, from what I understand. Let her in on some secrets. Miranda Everlast Thomas. Her boxes. Her lore." He shakes his head, as if some big piece in a puzzle he's been mulling has been settled into place. He forgets that I am here, seems to.

"So you really are Miss Martine's son," I say.

He smiles vaguely. "It seems you had established that."

"I mean, I was only guessing: from the photographs, the newspaper stories. The storm. Local Lore. Guessing from that."

He looks at me for a long time, then looks again at the photograph in his hand, which I'm sure he can hardly see by now, not where he's standing, not at this time of day. The stream sings its song and there's a rustling in the woods. Some lightning bugs have begun to put their lamps into the night. "This is the only formal portrait ever taken of my mother and father together," he says now. "I've been looking for it for a long time." He takes another long look at whatever part of the photo he can still see, then slips it in his pocket.

"The second gazebo?" I ask.

He nods. "I needed help," he says, "to move this earth around. It's old earth. It falls hard on itself."

"We were digging for this all along? A photo-graph?"

He nods again, shrugs. "My mother passed away last year," he says. "I wanted this back."

"Gone?" I step back, feel a shudder rip its way up my spine, think of Ida poking Reny, all the things folks keep to themselves.

"She died, Katie. Her time had come."

"Died?" I turn and look up at her house—through the trees, toward the mansion, where just that single light is on. I think about my mother's flowers blooming in the pachysandra patch for a ghost of a woman, an idea. I think of rescue. "But I thought . . ." I turn back around to look at Old Olson, but the shadows really are falling fast, and I can't read his eyes anymore. I wait for him to explain, to fit the pieces together, but he turns now, straightens a dahlia that has fallen lightly against its mesh cage. His gloves remain on the ground, where he tossed them. He keeps his back to me.

"Old Olson?" I say, finally.

"Listen, Katie," he says. He turns back around, crosses his arms, looks up at the sky, starts speaking. "It's just the way it is, okay? Just the way it was." This, I realize, is a story he hasn't often told. An entire history, long buried. "She had never been well, my mother," he starts again. "After she lost my father, and I was born. My first memories are of her being far away, of me, running down that hill"—he gestures—"tossing pebbles in the stream, hunting for fish, finding an owl. My mother near, but distant. They sent me to school after a while—her mother and her father, I mean. I'd come home for the summers, for Christmas, but mostly

I grew up in other places. Grew up loving this place, most of all. Grew up missing her."

"So you came back?"

"At one point, her father died, her mother was gone, and what was I going to do, really? Who could care for this place? She wasn't even forty, but she was frail. I was through with college. So yes, Katie. I came home. I stayed. She loved it here, despite everything, and when she wanted to leave, I took her. She wore scarves, big sunglasses, hats. No one was much looking for her anymore. Nobody noticed." His words are quiet. He doesn't move. A slight breeze moves through my hair. "Cancer," he says.

Cancer. A word we both understand.

"I thought she was still here," I say. "Up there." I point to the house, to the light on the hill. "I thought . . ."

"You thought what I wanted anyone who wondered to think. What everyone needed to think, if I was to stay here and still honor my mother's secret.

It was easier to let people imagine her alive. Easier to pass as her gardener than a son. We had lawyers who helped." He smiles. "The privilege of money."

Way above Old Olson's head, the first pale star has come out. Something quick and small moves through the air above—a couple of bats, maybe—and the dry, hot air of the day is starting to feel perforated with something sweeter. There are a million images in my head, a thousand questions.

"How did you know the portrait existed in the first place?" I ask him.

"At the very end she spoke of it. Said she'd had it hidden. I thought she meant that it had been locked in that trunk. I guess she meant that she had given it to Miranda. They'd had a falling-out after I was born. They weren't on speaking terms, long as I knew my mother."

"Then Miranda passed on."

"Then her son cleaned out her house."

"Then the boxes just looked like Local Lore," I say. "Like nobody special's story."

"I guess that's right." He touches the outline of the photo in his pocket. He settles his hip and bends his knee, like a man leaning up against a fence.

"What *is* in the trunk?" I ask.

"Everything she would have left with," he says, not bothering to make the mystery a mystery anymore, "had she had the freedom to leave."

"Where was she going?"

"To Virginia, with my father." He leaves it at that for a moment, lets the story hang, then continues. "They were planning to elope the night he died, and so she'd packed her trunk. There was a storm. She didn't care. She hired a taxi to take her to the train, but the taxi couldn't get far—rain everywhere, floods, splinters of trees on the ground, and the taxi stalled. My father boarded the train without her. Her father went to find her. Three days later, she learned my father was dead. When her father understood that she was carrying me, that she had planned to escape with a horseman, to elope, he buried her trunk in the ground. He didn't want a soul to find it, didn't want a trace of it anywhere. She was sixteen. Four months later I was born, and she didn't leave this place after that. It was said she'd gone to Europe. A lot of things, really, were said."

I nod, tip my chin to the sky, wipe a tear from my cheek. More stars have begun to appear and brighten. *Hello, Mom,* I think. *Hello, Miss Martine.* "So what is next?" I ask. "For you?"

"I'm leaving, Katie. Hurts too much to see the old place empty. Have lost my strength for it."

"And Ida and Reny, and Yvonne and Peter . . . ?"

"They'll stay with the new folks, if they want. Go off, if they want. They'll be able to choose; it'll be part of the terms."

I bite my lip. "That's nice of you," I say.

"They're family, Katie. That's what you do."

I nod again, and through the descending darkness I

see him smile. "I want to show you something, Katie," he says. He begins walking and I follow—down the path, under the trellis, toward the bridge where Danny and I stood in the dark and kissed. Seems like a long time ago. I stay three steps behind him, fitting my boots into his boot prints. Just short of the stream he stops and pulls back the branches of a big tree, and because it's all so shadowy out here right now, he takes my hand and lifts it up, against the bark, where I find the hard head of a nail.

"Turtle shell," he says.

I shake my head, don't understand.

"They'd rendezvous here by the tree," he says. "My mother and my father. The shell was their sign."

"So they hung it there? On a nail on a tree?"

"A story my mother loved to tell," he says. And then, out of nowhere, he laughs. An owl hoots back as if to answer, and now Old Olson laughs again.

Chapter *Thirty*

D ad's at work in the kitchen when I get home. "Good day at Miss Martine's?" he calls out, and I just say, "Hey." I don't know where I can start, and every inch of me is aching. Later tonight, I'll tell Dad the whole story, and after that I'll call Danny, and after that I'll sleep. The only thing I want right now is a long and steaming shower.

"Katie?" he says when I'm half up the stairs.

"Yeah?"

"Might as well get something decent on."

"What?"

"A dress or something. I don't know. I'm preparing one of my all-time specials."

"Dad," I say, "why don't we just have eggs, or toast? We could have cereal."

"No way," he says. "Not a single chance. I think I'm onto something."

I turn, and I'm sure the surprise is in my face. Coincidence, or a joke of his? Just his way of being Jimmy? "Onto something in the kitchen, or onto something with the painting?"

"Now what would be the fun of me telling you when you're all sourpussed like that?"

If I argued, or begged, my body would hurt even more. I give him an "okay" shrug and continue heading up the stairs and to my room and then down the hall, passing the room where the things that were my mother's were and, at least for now, still are. I turn the shower water to extra hot. I lose myself inside the steam.

By the time I make it back downstairs, I realize something's actually up. The living room is half as messy, for one thing, and the kitchen is basically scrubbed. Cooked in, but scrubbed. The extra leaf has been fitted into the table and a linen tablecloth thrown on, and on one end is the bud vase and on the other is a water pitcher stuffed full with black-eyed Susans. Dad's got one of Mom's aprons on, but he's also wearing a regular shirt with the sleeves rolled up an equal distance on his arms.

"Dad," I ask, "what's going on?"

"Well, don't you look lovely?" He tips his head in my direction when he turns to see me. "Your mother loved you in that dress, I remember."

"She bought it for me," I tell him. I spin, and the yellow skirt kicks out a circle.

"You look like a pinwheel."

I glance past him toward the sink, the counters, the top of the oven. He's grilled asparagus and sprinkled it with cheese. He's tossed blueberries and raspberries in with a salad. He's filled an oval plate with crackers and cheese. "You look like you've been cheffing all day," I tell him.

"Wait," he says, "until you see what I've got in the oven."

"What's going on?"

"We're having a party."

"We are?"

"Yes, and if you would be so kind as to set the table? Six settings, Katie, with the linen napkins."

I don't budge. "Dad. Seriously. What's going on?" I can't see how he's got a surprise when I'm the one who has solved the mystery, stumbled onto all the answers.

"We're having a party, like I said."

"Any particular reason?" I'm still standing, not

moving an inch. Dad lets out the longest, most theatrical sigh. He starts collecting the plates, the forks, the knives, the napkins, and presenting these.

"End-of-summer celebration."

I open my hands, take on the stack of table things, still don't budge. "It's not the end of summer, Dad."

"Oh, Katie," he says, "do you always have to be so right? Just go with this for a while."

"Six places, Dad?" I start laying things out.

"Well, will you look?" he says. "Here comes our first guest already."

I follow Dad's gaze, out the kitchen window, see Sammy Mack and Mrs. Mack, walking up like two civilized people. The kid's dressed just like a normal person—a pair of khakis, a dark blue tee, his light-up sneakers. He's holding his mother's hand. They knock, then let themselves in. Sammy breaks free from his mother's hold and runs toward my dad, giving him a friendly smack against the thigh.

"Awfully nice of you, Jimmy," Mrs. Mack says to my dad, then, to Sammy, "Your very best behavior now—remember what we talked about." Sammy pumps his head in his best imitation of agreeing.

"Thank you for bringing him over," Dad says. "We'll get him safely home later on." Mrs. Mack smiles at my dad, gives a stern look to her son. She waves at me like I'm a second thought, like she didn't actually see me until now.

"You remember my daughter, Katie," Dad says.

"Of course," she says, waving hello and good-bye.

"What's for dinner, Jimmy?" Sammy asks.

"Chicken," Dad says. "And spaghetti squash. It tastes just like spaghetti."

"Does it taste like pizza?"

"We could pretend."

Sammy sets off on a triumphal march, all around the kitchen, pumping his little fists, nodding his head, making his shoes light up like fireworks.

"Is it Sammy's birthday?" I ask my father.

"Not that I know of. Is it, Sammy?"

Humming to himself now, Sammy is off in his own world. I finish setting the table—forks on linen napkins, plates in their places, water glasses, knives. When I turn, I find Dad's next guest has slipped in so quietly that I hadn't even heard her. I'm too flabbergasted to say hello. Have you ever seen one of those cool Gap models in the pages of *Vanity Fair*? That's who she looks like—all funky but sweet, with the coolest, tallest pair of cranberry-colored shoes. "Ms. McDermott," I say, feeling my face turn red hot. "Dad didn't tell me you were coming—"

"She's tough to surprise," Dad interrupts. "I do my best." Even Sammy's stopped to give the librarian the once-all-over.

"Hello again," he says.

Again?

"Dad?" I start, but now there's another knocking

at the door, and I give Dad my are-you-crazy? look.

"Our final guest," Dad says.

I set off through the kitchen, practically skid into the door. When I yank it open, Danny's staring at me, a purple dahlia in his hand. "Are you kidding me?" I ask. I don't step aside to let him through. I just keep staring at him.

"Would I do that?"

"What?" I already forgot my question.

"Kid you?"

"What are you doing here?" I ask, and he's still outside and I'm still inside, and I have a million things to tell him, more than a million, and again there's this problem—I don't know where to start—and finally I remember to make some room.

"I was invited." He steps toward me. He stands there, slipping the purple dahlia into my hand.

"By my dad?" It's a perfect dahlia. I know precisely where he got it.

"By Ms. McDermott, actually. Who received the invitation by way of your dad and decided to include me. Cool house, by the way. Way big. Like a mini Miss Martine mansion."

"I'm so confused."

"Is this the famous Danny Santopolo?" It's my dad now, come out from the kitchen, wiping his hands dry on my mother's flowered apron. All of a sudden I realize something: My father got his hair cut. He hardly looks mad scientist tonight.

"Good to meet you, Dr. D'Amore."

"Hope you like spaghetti squash."

"Never had it."

"You've got to have spaghetti squash before you go to college," Dad tells him, clapping a hand on Danny's shoulder and leading him into the kitchen, leaving me to walk behind the two of them. "One of life's most pressing rules."

"Good to know," Danny says. He waves to me from

behind his back. I catch his fingers briefly in mine. Looking past the two of them, I can see Sammy still on his march and Ms. McDermott slicing the bread as if she's always worked in our kitchen. The chicken's out of the oven. The meal is practically served. Dad stands at Mom's place so that no one will sit there. I choose the chair next to Danny. We're seated.

"Will you do us the honor?" Dad asks Sammy, who has plopped down next to him.

"Blessings on our blossoms," Sammy shouts.

"Amen," Dad says.

"Amen," we echo.

"There's enough of everything for everyone," Dad says, scooping things onto people's plates, passing dishes.

"You're quite the cook," Ms. McDermott tells him, and looking around the table now, I see that what she says is true. Dad has become a master chef. He'd win top prize on any reality TV cooking show.

"I've decided that cooking is just another way of painting," Dad says, and I think; *Oh, Mom, I hope that you heard that. I hope you can see us all here right now, that you're sitting with us, at this table.* I feel Danny's hand reaching for mine. I squeeze his fingers tight.

"My dad don't ever cook," Sammy announces, and Danny laughs, and now Sammy shouts, "Pizza time," digging into the squash. Dad asks for the bread, then he asks for the butter. Ms. McDermott takes another helping of salad. Danny says, "Wait till I tell Owen," and I say, "Don't," and Sammy says, "Who's Owen?" By now Dad is getting around to his point, is clearing his throat, saying, "We have all been at work on the mysterious case of Miss Martine. Today, I understand, there's been a breakthrough."

I stare at Dad, completely baffled. I stare at Sammy, who has started to fidget. I look at Danny, remember this morning, him talking on the bridge with Old Olson, him going off into the thick of the trees. Danny,

I think—maybe Danny beat me to knowing, but now I realize, looking around the table again, that the person I should be watching is Ms. McDermott. There's a blush of high red in her cheeks, an expression on her face that I have never seen before. "I just happened to mention to your dad," she says, "that I bumped into you in the library today. That you'd had yourself a breakthrough."

"You told him that?"

"I did."

"But when?"

"When he called me to verify something about the painting."

"Which I'd shared with Ms. McDermott the night she came to drop off the photo of Miss Martine," Dad adds now. "The painting, I mean. I'd given her a tour."

"There's a painting?" Danny asks.

"I was planning to tell you," I say.

"And a photograph?"

"It's just that's all come together only now." I feel my cheeks go hot.

"But you were going to tell me?" Danny asks.

"I was. I can tell you now."

"What's going on?" Sammy shouts, impatiently, a funny look on his superhero face.

"I found a portrait," I say. "In box number seven. A portrait that tells the whole story. Or sort of most of it. The rest I got from Old Olson."

Ms. McDermott gives me a beautiful smile. My dad settles back into his chair. "Go on." I feel Danny's hand beneath the table, his fingers cool and gentle, forgiving, and now I learn forward and draw a deep breath, put the story in its place.

"Turns out that Miss Martine had a cousin," I begin. "But she was more than a cousin, really, I guess. More like Miss Martine's best friend. And some of the things that mattered most to Miss Martine were entrusted, for safekeeping, to the cousin."

"But what's the story?" Sammy shouts. He has crisscross marks on his forehead from paying so much attention.

"The story, Sammy, happened in September, right about this time of year, fifty-something years ago, which is thirteen of your lifetimes."

Sammy looks at me and smiles. Danny squeezes my hand. I continue. "In that night in that year, a big storm blew in from Florida, then rammed itself up the East Coast, then stayed. Streams got to be rivers, and rivers overflowed, and boats floated off and parked beside houses and the roofs of houses blew down, and a train that Miss Martine had been planning to take got thrown right off its tracks."

"You can't throw a train off its tracks," Sammy says.

"We use the word *derailed*, Sammy." I look from Sammy to Dad and back again. Then I look at Ms.

McDermott. Her eyes are full behind her glasses, eager, I realize, for the story.

"So where was she going?" Danny asks. "When the storm got in her way?"

"She was going to marry a man she loved. She was eloping."

"Who?" Dad asks.

"A horseman," I say. "By the name of Olson Long." I turn to Danny. "He was her trainer. Their love was a secret."

"Okay," he says. "Keep going."

"When they decided to elope, she packed her trunk, she snuck away, but the storm had set in," I continue. And now all of a sudden, as I am telling this story, I am right there with Miss Martine, right there in that night, in that storm, with a trunk packed full of everything a society queen would need to live with the man she loved, the father of her child. And the rains come down and they won't stop coming, and the winds blow and they won't stop blowing, and somewhere in the city, the man boards a train, and somewhere in the suburbs a taxi stalls, and sometime later that night that train will jump its tracks. It was John Butler Everlast who hurried out into the storm to find his daughter. Just him driving the washed-over roads, not his chauffeur. Just him beside the swollen river, desperate to save his daughter, first, and then, in his own way, to protect her. He took her home and buried her trunk full of things, and then he kept the secret of her baby. He brought her home, and that is where she stayed. Brokenhearted. Broken. Her son tending to her world.

Ms. McDermott shakes her head; the whole table's quiet. Even Sammy, down there, is quiet. "She never escaped," I say, "and she never really lived either. Her heart was broken. She was so young."

"So that's the story," Danny says after a moment of silence. "The way Old Olson tells it."

"And then there's the story," Dad says, "as Everlast

tells it. In his painting. He had to paint it right onto a canvas. His own disappointment, his deep regrets. Amazing, Katie. Amazing. The story. The way you found it."

"I just don't get why she had to vanish altogether," I say, thinking of Miss Martine in that house on the hill. "Why she had to lock herself away from the world. Why she didn't just step back into life, after a while."

"There's no way of knowing, Katie," Ms. McDermott says.

The before and the after, I think. The color of caution.

"The brutal politics of regret," Dad says.

"The politics of shame," Ms. McDermott says, shaking her head.

But I still can't see it. I still can't understand that kind of disappearance, one that you choose for yourself, like you're dead, but you're actually not, like you're a ghost, but you're still flesh and bones, like you want to live but cannot. Gone until the past got dug back up again.

Maybe love, I think, is the biggest thing there is. Maybe love also contains the most amount of ruin, and I look at my dad and my mom's empty chair, and I think about Danny going away in a few days, and I remember Jessie and Ellen and my own disappearing, and now I consider Ms. McDermott, going home every night to her house full of books, though she's the most stunning librarian there is and could have anyone she wanted, if she wanted to take that chance. Maybe loving once means some part of you is stuck loving forever—loving and chasing and living with whatever you're lucky enough to remember.

"We all come to terms," Dad says, "in our own time."

I sit beside Danny, knowing that my dad is right. I sit here imagining Miss Martine and my mother's flowers, settled in now, in her yard. I sit wondering if I'll ever come to terms with losing my one and only mother, and then I suddenly feel grateful for the things that I still have, and the new things, too.

"Pretty great party, Dad," I say, choking up.

"House needed a little livening up," Dad says. "And besides, who doesn't love a bona fide mystery?" He looks all right, almost half happy, one hand on the back of my mother's chair, one hand on the back of Ms. McDermott's. He takes a good long look at Sammy now and makes some kind of decision. "Katie, love," he says, "will you take my first-rate assistant home? He appears to be a tad kaput." I look toward that end of the table, and he's right: Sammy's half asleep—his eyes half open and his face all smeared, as if he has eaten way too much pizza.

"Everything was really great, Dr. D'Amore," Danny says, standing beside me. "I'm glad we've met."

"The door's pretty much always open at the

D'Amores'," Dad says. "I'm a great fan of Katie's friends." Danny makes the slightest bow. I give my dad a forehead kiss.

"Come on, Sammy," I say, reaching out my hand.

He shakes his head no and doesn't budge. Gently I wrestle him out of the chair, give him a kiss of his own.

"I'm coming back," he says with a perfect pout. "I'm coming back tomorrow."

"Breakfast will be waiting," I say.

Acknowledgments

I'm not sure that any of us ever come fully to terms with loss. And yet, in the stretch of time since my mother's passing, I've been given the gift of extraordinary friendship by a deeply appreciated many. My first thanks, then, go to all who listened and loved, who filled my home with cards and flowers, who showed the way. *Nothing but Ghosts* is filled with their essence—with the deep, faithful goodness of my father; with Jamie Comiskey's spaghetti squash; with the kindness of Yvonne D'Amore and Ann McDermott; with the pure alivedness of my nieces and nephews, Miranda, Owen, Julia, Daniel, and Claire; with the impeccable intelligence of Ivy Goodman, Alyson Hagy, Jennie Nash, Rahna Reiko Rizzuto, Kate Moses, Ellen Brackett, Amy Rennert, and my own aunt Carol. Jeremy: How you have taught me, inspired me, blessed me. Bill, thank you.

To the Harper team—Laura Geringer, Jill Santopolo, Corey Mallonee, Cindy Tamasi, Lisa Bishop, Carla Weise, Renée Cafiero, Laaren Brown—I thank you for all you do. Laura, especially, I thank you for standing by with this, for seeing more inside the lines than I had seen myself.

Chanticleer Garden and the souls who keep it blooming: Once again, you have planted seeds; you have given this story a most glorious physical home.